ABOUT THIS BOOK

HADDER MacCOLL
Patricia Calvert

Hadder MacColl, fourteen-year-old daughter of the fiery Highlands chieftain Big Archibald, cannot believe that her brother's
three years of study at Edinburgh have changed him so. She
can remember waking up every morning, throwing their saddles on the backs of their horses, and riding like the wind
across the moors behind their father's house. They both had
yearned for the day when Bonnie Prince Charlie would return
from exile and the clans would rally behind him. Together
they would join the battle and rout the English to win back the
crown of his ancestors. Now the prince has landed on the
coast, but Hadder's beloved brother no longer wants to fight.
Only the honor of Big Archibald drives him to follow the
clans. Oh, if only Hadder could go to war! She'd show them
what it means to be a child of Big Archibald MacColl....

Hadder MacColl

BY PATRICIA CALVERT

Puffin Books

PUFFIN BOOKS

Viking Penguin Inc., 40 West 23rd Street, New York, New York 10010, U.S.A.
Penguin Books Ltd, Harmondsworth, Middlesex, England
Penguin Books Australia Ltd, Ringwood, Victoria, Australia
Penguin Books Canada Limited, 2801 John Street, Markham,
Ontario, Canada L3R 1B4
Penguin Books (N.Z.) Ltd, 182–190 Wairau Road, Auckland 10, New Zealand

First published by Charles Scribner's Sons 1985
Published in Puffin Books 1986
Copyright © Patricia Calvert, 1985
All rights reserved
Printed in U.S.A. by R. R. Donnelley & Sons Company, Harrisonburg, Virginia
Set in Caslon 540

Library of Congress Cataloging in Publication Data
Calvert, Patricia.   Hadder MacColl.
Summary: Fiercely proud and loyal to her Highland heritage, fifteen-year-old
Hadder can't understand why her beloved older brother, after his return
from schooling in Edinburgh, no longer seems to share her passionate belief
in the Jacobite cause.
1. Jacobite Rebellion, 1745–1746—Juvenile fiction.   2. Culloden, Battle of,
1746—Juvenile fiction.   [1. Jacobite Rebellion, 1745–1746—Fiction.
2. Culloden, Battle of, 1746—Fiction.   3. Scotland—History—18th
century—Fiction]   I. Title.   [PZ7.C139Had   1986]   [Fic]
86-4878   ISBN 0-14-032158-6

For my parents,
Helen Patricia Frank
and
Edgar Clyde Dunlap,
with love

Gather up the fragments that remain,
that nothing be lost.

—JOHN 6:12

FOREWORD

During a rainstorm on Friday, July 23, 1745, a young man landed with seven companions on the lonely island of Eriskay, a few miles off the west coast of Scotland. He was the youngest prince of the house of Stuart, and although he arrived without militia or muskets or horses for a cavalry, he came with rebellion in his heart.

Charles Edward Stuart, or Bonnie Prince Charlie, as Scots Highlanders called him, was determined to win back the crown for his father, James, whose own father, James II, had been exiled to France in 1689. The prince's plan was simple: he would raise an army from the loyal Stuart clans, clans with names that rang like bells in Scots history—Mac-Donald and MacLean, Fraser and Farquharson, Cameron and MacColl.

There had been other Stuart rebellions, of course, for the union between Scotland and England had always been an uneasy alliance. But the Rising of the Forty-Five, as Prince Charlie's rebellion was named, was unique because it divided the loyalties of Scotland itself and pitted clan against clan, father against son, brother against brother.

When the rebellion was over, Prince Charlie was immortalized in folksong and legend. The fate of the clansmen who drew their swords and came riding over the heather on their tough Highland ponies to rally around the Stuart banner has less often been celebrated in song or story.

Yet there are times when the wind rises near Ballachulish, or on certain afternoons when the blooming purple heather smells like honey in the sun, that folk who live in the Highlands are sure they can still hear the wild, clear cry of a girl named Hadder MacColl, can even hear the echoing hoofbeats of the bold red horse she rode away to war. . . .

1

"Stir your bones, Hadder," Glenisha whispered in my ear.
She pressed a small, urgent hand against my shoulder. "Can
it be that my cheelie has slept so soundly she's forgotten
what day this is?"

I pulled the covers over my head. It's just another day
as dull as all of them have been since Leofwin went away,
I wanted to remind her. Instead, I grumbled crossly from
the warm, bogley dark of my blanket cave, "Let me be,
Glenisha! Let me sleep and dream. . . ."

I would dream, of course, of Leofwin. I shaped his name
silently with my lips, and the taste of it on my tongue was
sweeter by far than the strawberries Glenisha and I gathered
every summer at the edge of the glen.

My brother's name, which is Gaelic, was settled on him
by our mother, and it means to win love. When it is spoken,
the first two vowels are run smoothly together, the *e* no
more bold than the *o*, so that the sound that is uttered is
softer than the sigh of a Highland wind through the trees:
luff-win, luff-win.

Then, with my brother's name still on my lips, I came wide awake. I realized why Glenisha had taken pains to rouse me so early. I had waited impatiently for this day for three long years—but when it arrived I'd slept late like an enchanted girl in a fable! Today, after having been sent away to study subjects like mathematics and history and philosophy in the city of Edinburgh, Leofwin was coming home to stay.

I hugged myself in the delicious darkness of my bed-clothes. When Leofwin was home again in Ballachulish where he belonged, the pain of his absence would vanish as if it'd never been. Every morning, as had been our habit in days gone by, we would throw our saddles on the backs of our horses and would ride like reivers across the moor that stretched behind the house of our father, Big Archibald of the Strong Blows, the chief of Clan MacColl.

Bound to each other by a pledge we'd sealed in blood, Leofwin and I would once again hunt down red deer for our father's table. We would flush fat, speckled grouse out of the heather. We would fish for salmon that ran like silver ribbons in the foamy waters of the firth. Best of all, I would never be lonely again.

And maybe Leofwin would even agree to travel with me into the woods so we could forge our pledge anew. We would ride together down a certain narrow trail known only to us. Along its borders deer sedge grew in tufted patches; violets and eyebrights bloomed in the dusky shadows; the air was always sweet with the smell of pine.

When we reached the heart of the forest, we would pause beside a small, dark pool. It was there, as our reflected selves watched from the black water, that Leofwin and I had pricked our fingers with a dirk. We had mingled our blood and promised to be true to each other and to the honor of Clan MacColl. Leofwin had looked up at the trees that arched above our heads and whispered to me, "With this pledge, we are bound together forever—and we'll call this place the Forest of Forever!"

Ah, Leofwin, Leofwin! My brother's name did indeed mean to win love, but I was fourteen when he came home to Ballachulish in 1745, and I had already loved him all my life.

I threw off my covers and vaulted out of bed. "Leofwin's coming home today!" I shouted at Glenisha, as if it was she who'd foolishly forgotten that fact and needed reminding, rather than the other way around.

I seized her in my arms and hugged her—not too briskly, of course, for Glenisha is bruckle, as we say in the Highlands, or somewhat frail. She is as small as a child, and her gauzy hair is the same pale color as the cotton grass we harvest every autumn and use to make our lampwicks.

Through my thin chemise, Glenisha's old bones against my own felt as delicate as the limbs of the china doll my mother brought home to me from Edinburgh when I was eight. My mother, who came to my father's house from Clan Donald of Glencoe, had longed for a quiet daughter, a girl who'd be happy to learn weaving and the art of managing the home of a clan chief. But of all the girls who'd ever lived in Ballachulish, either highborn or lowborn, I was the one least likely to care for such things—or ever to have wanted a doll!

4

Glenisha struggled out of my arms, and her cheeks turned pink where the bone came close to the skin. "How you take on!" she scolded, pleased in spite of herself by my rough attention. "Out of that shift, cheelie," she went on, "and into something pretty for a change!" Glenisha, too, wished for me to be someone I knew I was not.

"There's no telling exactly what hour Leofwin will arrive," she fussed, "so I advise you to look your best the whole day long. But one of the Camerons from Lochiel came riding by only yesterday and reported that your brother had been seen near Achallader, so that means he might be—"

"—here before noon!" I finished for her, so loudly that she covered her ears. The wood floor under my bare feet was cool as I splashed water over my face and dried it on the coarse towel Glenisha held out to me. It was April, but a chill still lay everywhere. Warm weather would not come to the Highlands for at least two months more, and even when it did, we would still welcome warm coats as soon as the sun went down.

I shivered my way into a clean linen shirt, pulled on a wool skirt, and drew on a pair of warm moggans, or stockings. I fastened the brass buckles on my shoes. To please Glenisha, I had not chosen a pair of ordinary brogues for my feet and did not annoy her by lacing rough deerskin buskins up to my knees. Then I settled myself on a low stool in front of my old minnie so that she could brush out my hair. In the Highlands, a minnie is a mother, and that is exactly what faithful Glenisha had been to me for longer than I wanted to remember.

"Wild and snarly as a moor pony's tail!" she declared as she brushed my long hair. I didn't mind her words. She'd said the same ones to me nearly every morning since my mother died five long years ago. To complain to me was Glenisha's way of telling me that she cared—together with often calling me cheelie, "dear child."

We of the Highlands are careful with our affections. Oh, in a moment of rare weakness my father had indeed allowed my mother to settle on her firstborn a name that meant to win love, but the truth is that we of the high country all are proud of being as hard as the stones that lie beneath the thin soil of our mountains. In long ago times, our newborn were dipped into the icy waters of a loch, then held aloft and turned three times around a fire. Such a custom has guaranteed that even now we do not yield readily to softness.

That was why, when the moment came to send his only son away, Big Archibald knew there was no real danger to it. No one in the whole city of Edinburgh had the power to soften Leofwin's heart, of that my father was certain! Of course, the unwelcome fact that my brother would one day have to leave the Highlands was something we'd always known.

Long before either Leofwin or I was born, when the parliaments of England and Scotland were united in 1707, the Privy Council of Edinburgh—which was made up of men from both nations—decreed that any clan chief who owned more than sixty cattle (Big Archibald had ten times that many!) must send his sons away to be educated far outside the Highlands.

6

Our wealth, you see, was measured in cattle, and by teaching history and mathematics and philosophy to the sons of cattle-rich clan chiefs, the English and their Lowland friends hoped they could eventually tame our fierce spirit. They had always lived in mortal fear of the Lions of the North, as they liked to call the people of the clans.

"Not that we have ever made it easy for them to feel otherwise!" Big Archibald liked to exclaim with pride. Since we were impoverished by the sour soil of the high country, which did not bear fine crops, and since we were prohibited by the English from trading our leather and wool and cattle with countries across the seas, we of the Highlands had for many years earned our livelihood by raiding our neighbors in the Lowlands.

We lifted corn and barley and oats in our forays against southern farms and villages. As long as we'd made the trip, we also helped ourselves to our neighbors' cattle and horses and sheep. If we'd not yet burdened ourselves overmuch with plunder, we cobbed their pots and pans and linens as well. My uncle, Black John MacDonald, once took a fancy to a handsome window of rose-colored glass that was set in a Lowland house—so he pulled it out and carried it all the way home to Glencoe on the back of his horse!

Once, dressed as a lad, I went on a raid with my father and brother. I cobbed myself a bridle with flowers carved in its leather cheek-straps. Leofwin told me those flowers were Spanish roses. "Someday I will steal a horse worthy to wear such a bridle!" I promised him. When I did, though, I would disguise myself as a lad again. Even in the wild Highlands, it was not proper for a girl to behave as I did,

7

no matter if she was the daughter of Big Archibald MacColl of Ballachulish.

Our habits caused us to be called outlaws and thieves and reivers by outsiders, but Big Archibald had a quick reply for such charges. "What is called a crime in Edinburgh is only the settlement of an old debt to a Highlander," he would retort with a sly wink.

On a few of their raids, my father and Leofwin had carried away books and newspapers from Lowland homes, and it was from them that I learned about the colonies that called themselves America. After my brother went to Edinburgh, Big Archibald taught me how to read and write, as he once had taught Leofwin. I learned how to use a map and studied the history of such famous Scots battles as Bannockburn in 1314 and Glenfruin in 1602. My father himself had been sent by his father to be educated in places like Paris and Rome and had returned to the Highlands with a foxy gloss to his rough ways. He also fetched home silver drinking cups and tapestries of blue and green and gold for his bride, Barbara MacDonald of Glencoe.

But when the grayheads of Edinburgh became truly distressed by our thieving ways, Letters of Fire and Sword were issued against us. Sometimes a man even was judged to be an outlaw and was put to the horn. Such action once had been taken against my father: his name was read aloud at Mercat Crossing, a horn was sounded three times, and he was declared thenceforth to be broken, or outside the law. *Hah!* There was no way for those feeble old men of Edinburgh ever to break a man like Big Archibald of the Strong Blows!

Yet in spite of the faith my father had in the hardness of

Leofwin's heart, he did not take lightly the sending of his only son so far from Ballachulish. When Big Archibald spoke bitterly of the matter over a supper of roast venison one evening, I decided the time had come to have a say myself.

"Send me!" I challenged him. "I'll go to Edinburgh in Leofwin's place!"

After all, I'd gone on a raid, hadn't I? And stolen a bridle decorated with Spanish roses? That deed made me the equal of any boy! At my offer, Big Archibald smiled widely and reached out to give my hair a pull. Perhaps he meant to tease me and tug it gently, but he succeeded in giving me a tweak that brought water to my eyes.

I leaped up from my bench, threw down my knife so hard it stuck point-first in the oak table at which we ate. In a temper I hurled my piece of roast venison halfway across the room. The meat struck the mantel above the fireplace and fell to the stone floor with a soggy smack. The venison had been cooked rare, the way Big Archibald liked it best, and scarlet drops rained across the snowy linen cloth that Glenisha had spread for us.

"Don't mock me," I shouted, "for if Leofwin must be sent away, then so should I!" It was my fondest dream: that Leofwin and I would be sent away to Edinburgh together and would never have to be parted.

My father laughed at my outburst, his great lion's head thrown back, his square white teeth agleam between his chapped red lips. Leofwin reproved me with a mild glance from under a pair of raised golden brows and kept right on eating.

"We couldn't send *you*, Mary Hadder MacColl," my

father roared. He wiped his lips gleefully on the sleeve of his coat. "You're a brimmer, lass, that's why!" My temper amused him and caused him none of the grief it had caused my mother. He covered my hand with his own large paw and squeezed it hard. "Edinburgh Castle and Holyrood House wouldn't be safe against the likes of you, for you are a fiercer cub even than your brother!"

Well, it was quite true that I was not faithful to the name that my mother had chosen for me. She had wanted her firstborn to win love, and when I was born four years later, had named me Mary, which means exalted. But I wasn't! And while Leofwin got our mother's yellow curls and eyes that were the color of gentians, I got our father's fiery hair and eyes that were as broody and black as spent coals.

When Glenisha finished her brushing at last, she tossed a burr into my lap. "Your father has one son," she reminded me, as if all the time she'd been brushing my hair she'd been peering into my head and reading my thoughts, "and he doesn't need two!" She laid my plaited hair over my left shoulder, as is often the custom among the girls of Ballachulish. I tossed the braid aside so that it hung straight down my spine like the tail of one of the moor ponies that Glenisha seemed to despise.

But she could not resist one last attempt to civilize me. She leaned close and whispered in my ear: "Perhaps Leofwin will bring you something from Edinburgh, cheelie. Something shiny or soft to help you remember you're a lass, not a lad!"

For a moment the notion charmed me. Might my brother bring me a cameo brooch filigreed with gold to wear on my new deerskin vest? Or maybe a shirt of lime-green silk to lie against my skin as light as summer air? Would such bribes make me wish to be called Mary instead of Hadder, as I had always insisted I be?

It was not a risk I was ready to take. I leaped up from my stool. "There's only one gift that Leofwin needs to bring home," I declared loudly. "Only himself! He's all that I want—now or ever!" For to know that my brother was home where he belonged, to ride with him once again through the forests and across the moors of the Highlands, was all that mattered to me.

3

As soon as I had eaten the breakfast of cold potatoes and boiled herring that Glenisha set out for me and had washed it all down with two cups of hot, dark tea sweetened with wild honey, I hurried outside to fly across the moor that stretched behind my father's house.

I turned back once, before the mist made it hard for me to see, to view the house where I'd been born and my father before me and his father before that. We were all descended from Colla, Prince of the Isles, and the placement of *Mac* in front of our name was a way of saying to the world: these are the sons and daughters of Coll.

The sight of the home of the children of Coll never failed to surprise me: its whitewashed walls rose softly pale and tall into the morning mist, the sharp peaks of its blue slate roof burnished with golden lichens. In all the whole wide landscape, my father's house was the only white object to be seen, and because it was also three stories tall, it was often called the White Tower by his tacksmen.

East of the tower rose the great blue tumble of the mountains of Glencoe, the "glen of weeping." In those distant mountain valleys Clan Campbell fell upon the MacDonalds, my mother's people, on a cold February morning in 1692. Campbells murdered MacDonalds by the dozens, men and women and children alike, and stained the snow scarlet with their blood. We of the clans are so fierce and jealous that we quarrel not only with Lowlanders and Englishmen but with each other as well.

To the north of my father's house were the peaks of Ardgour. West lay the waters of Loch Linnhe, as blinding as a sheet of silver when the weather was fine, and fringed in summer with golden saffron weeds from which we made dye for our plaids. On the horizon where the sea met the sky loomed the dark blue heights of the Isle of Mull. Far beyond that was the Isle of Coll, where many of my ancestors lay buried. Oh, such sights I could never take for granted! They were carved on my heart just as Spanish roses were carved on the cheek-straps of my stolen bridle.

I turned away and once again hurried across the heath. Yet I needn't have walked to meet Leofwin. I could just as well have chosen to saddle up any one of the garrons that Big Archibald kept in his stable. These small, dun-colored horses are native to our Highlands; they thrive on pastures that would surely starve less hardy animals. One of my favorites from my father's herd was a trim little mare named Luath, the swift one.

But this morning I wanted to travel on foot, the better to take Leofwin by surprise. If I went on horseback, spunky Luath might whinny an eager greeting, and for a reason I could not explain even to myself, I wanted to see my brother before he saw me.

At the edge of the moor, on the side that faced away

Loch Linnhe, I stepped across a brook that rose out of the heather and skipped like a silver thief into the woods beyond. I hesitated. Leofwin would ride home on the cart road that came from the east. But noon was still hours away, I told myself. I had plenty of time to spare. I decided to follow the stream deeper into the woods.

The creek boiled like cream over smooth stones of pink and blue and white, but what made it dear to me was that it ran beside a path that was known only to Leofwin and me. In less than an hour I found myself once again beside the dark pool in the heart of the forest. It was the place where Leofwin and I had made our pledge so long ago and to which we'd given a special name.

A few curled leaves from the previous autumn still floated like golden boats on the dark water, high at their sterns and prows, ready for a mysterious journey. "When I turn my back," I wondered out loud, "will kelpies swim out from shore, climb into those boats, and sail away to find where the sun has gone?"

My wool skirt began to gather dew from the sedge, and mist that was caught in the tree branches above my head began to weep into my hair. But it was I who'd wept like any silly girl the day Leofwin rode away on Birkie, his dun-colored pony.

"Don't you realize what's happened, Haddie?" he'd asked me gently. My only answer had been to put my face in my hands and try to hide the tears I was so ashamed of.

"We aren't children anymore, Had," he explained softly, as if he wanted to spare my heart some terrible truth. "We grew up, one day at a time, until all those days were strung

14

together like beads on a string. That's what happened, Haddie. We just grew up."

His words made growing up sound like a death. I knew it couldn't be true. It was only the pain of leaving that made him imagine such a thing. Why, when we'd mingled our blood and promised to be true to each other, it was Leofwin himself who'd said to me: "With this pledge, we are bound together forever—and we'll call this place the Forest of Forever!"

Forever. The word turned inside my head like a great golden wheel, *foreverforeverforever*. I gave a merry wave to my reflection in the dark water, then ran up the path to meet my brother on the cart road that came from the east.

I heard Leofwin's voice before I caught my first sight of him. It had the same lilt as before but seemed deeper and more commanding than I remembered it to be. "But if he travels alone," I asked myself, "what need does he have to speak at all?" I jumped back from my place at the roadside and flattened myself into the damp heather.

The lad who faced me as he came over the rise in the road was not Leofwin at all.

He was a slender boy, not nearly as handsome as my brother, and he seemed closer to my age than to Leofwin's. His hair was the color of sunburned grass. He rode a clumsy brown horse with knobbed knees and white socks, and the miserable way he sat his mount made me suspect he was a lad who'd spent little time in a saddle.

Then, over the rise, came the one I had waited three long years to see again. It was Leofwin, astride Birkie, the same tough dun-colored pony that'd carried him out of the Highlands. But following him, led by the reins of a common leather bridle, came a tall, straight-legged, light-boned horse whose mane and tail were filled with wind, and whose fiery hide was exactly the color of my own wild hair.

What a scoundrel, I thought with delight. Leofwin has relieved some arrogant Lowland duke or earl of a handsome red horse and has fetched it home to the high country. I jumped out of the heather and barred the road with my fists set on my hips.

"Tread no farther!" I warned with pretended outrage. "This is MacColl country, and strangers proceed here at their peril!" Whereupon the stranger on his brown horse blanched with alarm, and his mount shied off the road to stumble into an elderberry thicket, its eyes white-cornered and wild.

Leofwin cocked his head and smiled widely, just as I'd known he would, and his teeth were as white as Big Archibald's. Seen up close, my brother's hair was more golden than I remembered, and the quickening in my chest told me that I loved him even better than before.

Leofwin edged his pony close to me and placed his hand, fingers spread fanwise, like a cap over my head. "Is this the little toe-rag I left behind so long ago?" he mocked, and I knew from the smile in his eyes that he loved me, too.

"No," he marveled, half to me and half to himself, "this must be the daughter of some other clan chief! This girl wears buckled shoes instead of brogues and her hair is braided and tidy! No, *this* cannot be Big Archibald MacColl's daughter. . . ."

I was sorry that I had let Glenisha shame me into trying to be something other than what I knew myself to be. Leofwin had called me a toe-rag, or a wild child, and that is what I truly was. He had been gone for three years but could still see it! He knew as well as I did that I would never be tame and pudding-faced like some other girls who lived in Ballachulish.

Leofwin's pony turned its face to mine and breathed sweetly against my cheek. My brother leaned across Birkie's neck. "Are you sure you want to throw me off the road, lassie?" he asked. "I've brought you a giftie; don't you first want to know what it might be?"

I stared up at him. His face was lean, and there was a hollow in each cheek that hadn't been there three years ago. He wore side-whiskers, too, and gentians would have envied the blueness of the eyes that looked into mine.

"I love you," I whispered, "and you are the only gift that I want."

The words were out before I could call them back, to my regret, for they caused Leofwin's smile to fade. He straightened himself quickly in his saddle and regarded me with an astonished glance. Oh, to love was one thing—but to speak of it as boldly as I had just dared to do was quite another!

"Well, then, tell me quick what sort of a gift you've fetched," I demanded loudly to cover my dismay. "Not a doll, I hope—nor a brooch nor a green silk shirt!" To my relief, Leofwin's wide, white smile came back as suddenly as it had flown.

"Aye, now don't I know a certain toe-rag better than that?" he teased. He held out to me the plain leather reins by which he led the red horse. "*This* is what I've fetched home for you, Hadder MacColl—a horse to match the color of your hair! Take him, lass; he's yours. . . ."

Leofwin laid the narrow reins across my open palm. A horse that was my own . . . not a common garron that I had to chose willy-nilly from Big Archibald's stable . . . a horse worthy enough to wear a bridle decorated with Spanish roses. I stepped past my brother unable yet to say a word of thanks. I was dimly aware that now the stranger on his brown horse had clambered back onto the road and was watching me, too.

Leofwin's gift to me was bonnier by far than anything I'd ever seen before. The horse's eyes were large, well-set in its head, and shone with a deep, dark fire. There was a sworl of crisp white hairs in its forehead that formed a four-pointed star, and rather than hanging loosely, its fore-lock had been neatly plaited and was tied with a green silk ribbon.

"What name is he called by?" I asked Leofwin, still amazed by my good fortune. The horse pricked its ears forward attentively at the sound of my voice and pressed its soft muzzle against my arm. "He's called Sionnach," Leofwin told me. Sionnach—a perfect name! *Shoo-nuck*, or a red fox, and that is certainly what he was.

"What sort of faint-hearted Lowlander did you cob him

from?" I asked Leofwin with a sly wink. To my surprise, I saw my brother's cheeks flush brightly, and out of the tail of my eye I could see that the straw-haired stranger gave both of us a quizzical glance.

"Why, I *bought* him for you, Haddie," Leofwin explained in a low voice. "For months, I bought no new books for my studies, and I ate cabbage every day, just so I could save the money to buy him for you! I didn't steal him in any raid. This horse comes to you honestly, Had."

Just why Leofwin believed the fact that the red horse had been gotten honestly would make him more precious to me was a puzzle. I was of the same opinion as Big Archibald about the settlement of old debts. Nevertheless, I gathered the fox-horse's reins close to its neck and prepared to mount.

Leofwin stayed me with a hand laid on my shoulder. "Before you throw a leg across that fine red back, Haddie, I want you to meet my friend." He gestured toward the boy on the brown horse. "This is David Forbes from Edinburgh, Had. David's father was my philosophy teacher. I've had many a meal at the Forbes' table, and now I want to return the kindness. David will be staying with us until we come home from the shielings in November."

From May to November every year we of the clans go to live in shielings, small stone cottages on the eastern moors, while we graze our cattle in their summer pastures. It was a time all of us loved, but I did not necessarily want to share it with a stranger. I glanced over my shoulder and allowed the newcomer a miser's stingy appraisal. David Forbes. A dull name. No bells rang in it.

Worse, for three whole years he'd been closer to Leofwin than I had been, and now we were to be a cozy threesome all summer! My first glance had been enough to tell me that Leofwin's friend had scorched hair that stuck out from under his cap like a tinker's. Now, on second glance, I could see that his eyes were pale and scared and his face was as narrow as a ferret's.

"You won't like life in the Highlands," I promised him coolly and vowed privately that I would find a way to make him glad to leave the mountains at his earliest opportunity.

I bent down, caught the back hem of my skirt in my right hand, drew it neatly between my knees, pulled it up, and tucked it snugly into my waistband. It had taken only a moment to make myself a pair of breeches. Next I seized a fistful of red mane and jumped onto the back of my fine red horse. Leofwin laughed at my nimbleness, but his friend spoke up with alarm.

"Leofwin, that horse might not be . . . that is, perhaps your sister shouldn't—"

"Shouldn't what, Mr. Forbes?" I demanded and insulted him with my eyes.

"You needn't worry, David," Leofwin assured his friend. "Hadder can stick like a star-burr to the back of any horse she rides. Remember, when we left Edinburgh I warned you that *my* sister was not at all like *your* sister!"

Ah, I mused, so David Forbes has a sister, a sister Leofwin knows rather well, from the sound of it all. The notion made my heart feel as dark and hard as a beechnut. She was a girl who'd be pale and pinched, I was sure. Her nose would be long and sharp, and she'd look as much like a ferret as her poor, frightened brother. Leofwin could not possibly care much for such a person.

I shouldered Sionnach impudently against David Forbes'

smaller brown horse. Mr. Forbes watched my approach with anxious eyes. "Your s-s-s-sister is a v-v-v-vauntie lass," he stammered to Leofwin as if trying to make a joke. Or had he meant the words unkindly? I shrugged, pleased to take them as a compliment, for I *was* bold, and I hoped he'd never forget that fact.

"Big Archibald is waiting," I told both boys, "so let's race all the way home to Ballachulish!" Sionnach moved between my knees as though we'd been paired together forever. We danced sideways down the narrow cart road while the two lads gathered their reins, then we were all flying across the heather, scattering aside the thin April mist that still shrouded the countryside. "Catch me if you can!" I cried over my shoulder.

But of course they couldn't. I was lighter and rode without a saddle and stayed far in the lead. Yet it was more than that; it was red Sionnach himself. I'd stuck like a burr to the back of many a spunky garron, just as Leofwin had boasted to David Forbes, but this horse was different. He might have been bought in Edinburgh, but he had a hard Highland heart, just like my own.

I raised a closed fist into the air and cried out the *pibroch*, the battle call of my father's clan: "We are strong and not afraid to die, and will pull our thunder from the sky!" Sionnach's bright mane filled with wind and lashed my cheeks, and I was glad that Leofwin had not brought me something shiny or soft as Glenisha had hoped, or anything else that would make me think I was like other girls. I was Hadder MacColl, a wild child, never to be mistaken for any poor, pale-necked thing who lived in Edinburgh.

22

5

Glenisha made rabbit soup for our supper. We downed huge bowls of it and mopped each one clean with pieces of warm barley bread slathered with cream cheese. I drank buttermilk, but Big Archibald and the lads drank silver tankards of nettle beer, a potion we fermented in springtime from young nettles, dandelions, and ginger. To startle our palates at the end of our meal, Glenisha served my favorite dessert, long pudding, made with plenty of suet and lots of lemon peel.

When we were done, Big Archibald leaned against the whitewashed stone wall behind him, laced ten fingers that were thick as sausages across his wide belly, and gave us a mighty belch. Relieved, he began at once to discuss what I knew to be his favorite topic. It was one he liked to chew as a dog chews a bone, and I squirmed on my hard bench, for I wanted to be up and gone to visit Sionnach one last time before it was too dark outside to see.

"Have you heard the rumor that's running like a fever through our hills, laddie?" my father asked Leofwin. My brother shook his golden head and Big Archibald boomed on. "They say our prince might come home to the Highlands! Aye, won't it be a great day when we take Scotland back for the Scots? And when the Stuart banner is raised, lad, we MacColls will rally round it along with the Camerons and the Frasers and the MacLeans!"

We MacColls—how I liked the good stout sound of that! So I was surprised indeed to see Leofwin fold his arms carefully against the edge of the table and lean toward my father. It seemed to me that he was thinking about the matter altogether harder than he needed to. "What, exactly, do you think the prince plans to do when he comes back?" my brother inquired, and with one forefinger idly began to trace a pattern on the cloth Glenisha had laid across our table.

"Plan to do?" Big Archibald echoed, even more amazed than I was. He squeezed his black eyes to tiny slits in his ruddy face. "Why, laddie, he plans to savage the English and their Lowland friends," he explained, as if Leofwin suddenly had gone dim in the head. "He intends to harry their cattle and scowder their fields! The lords of London and their Lowland cronies have tried for four hundred years to change the way we of the clans live—and I, for one, believe the time has come to dye the heather red with their blood and feed their hearts to the eagles—just to remind them it cannot be done!"

My father relished the fierce poetry of such remarks, as I did myself, but I was alarmed that he made them in front of a person like David Forbes. For all we knew, the boy might be a spy sent into our midst. The government in Edinburgh had sent such persons among us before, disguised as mail carriers or census-takers or clergymen. Why not disguise one as a student? I was sure that when I met a spy, he would have exactly the kind of narrow, ferret face as the one that belonged to David Forbes.

Leofwin did not match glances with my father. Instead, he smoothed out the pattern he'd drawn in the cloth and made it afresh. "I am not sure the prince knows as much as he ought to about the Highlands," my brother mused. "Scotland might indeed be the home of the prince's ancestors," he admitted, "but the man himself has never before set foot on our shores. What he knows far better than Scotland, I fear, are the courts of Paris and Rome."

For my father, who had been twenty years old when he fought in the last Stuart rising in 1719 and who had always longed for another, such second thoughts about the prince's character were treasonous. He unlaced his thick fingers and drew himself as upright as a shepherd's staff.

"Our prince is the son of James who was the son of James who was the son of Charles!" Big Archibald roared indignantly. "Of course the young man knows Scotland! Why, the land and its spirit are in his blood, just as they are in yours and mine!" *Mine, too!* I longed to shout. "Charles Edward Stuart is the son of our rightful king, Leofwin! It is James who should warm the throne now occupied by that Hanoverian dunce in London who has no taste for poetry, no heart for attachment, no soul for honor!"

I tossed a stealthy glance in David Forbes' direction. His eyes were fastened attentively on his empty soup bowl

25

as if it contained such rare delights as rabbit hearts and pheasant gizzards. All the same, I was sure he was listening to every word and would be quick to repeat everything the moment he returned to Edinburgh.

"Perhaps there are methods other than rebellion that would achieve what we want for the Highlands," Leofwin persisted. Before he went away to school, my brother had delighted in matching Big Archibald roar for roar. Now his voice was measured and low, and two tight white lines ran like scars from the corners of his lips to his chin.

"The heather has been dyed scarlet so many times in the past," he reasoned in his new and tactful way, reflecting no doubt on the rebellions of 1715 and 1719, "but the world is changing, Father. There are new trade routes opening to the colonies of America and to Africa and India as well. Maybe we can agree with the English to—"

"Never!" Big Archibald thundered, outraged by that word *agree*. "Not as long as there are leaves in the forest or foam on the river!" Then, as if he'd only been playing a game or baiting an old bear, my brother smiled his sudden wide, white lion's smile. "Quite so, sir!" he thundered in reply. "And when the prince comes, the clans will rise up from the glens and ride down from the bens, and the sun will shine like watered silver on their swords!"

It was precisely the kind of poetry my father wanted to hear. He beamed, and at that break in our conversation Glenisha crept among us to clear the table of its bowls and tankards. Big Archibald, as pleased as I was that Leofwin had come so quickly to his senses, belched one last time and hoisted himself away from the table.

26

"In two weeks we will start our journey to the shielings," he growled at us through a yawn. "Tomorrow you three must go out and hunt deer so that we will have plenty of fresh meat to carry with us." He motioned us to follow him upstairs to bed. I lingered a moment after the lads were gone to help Glenisha snuff the candles and to inspect the pattern Leofwin had drawn in the cloth on the table. It was the image of the letter *E*. Was he so fond of the city of Edinburgh that he wrote its initial in idle moments? I wondered. I smoothed the letter away with my finger and hurried up the narrow passageway, and soon the whole house was quiet.

I lay in bed fully dressed and waited until I could hear Big Archibald snoring steadily before I threw off my covers. The mist of the morning had cleared away, and now moonlight lay in silver ingots on the cold wood floor of my room. I pulled on a pair of common brogues and reached for my long wool coat.

From a small oak chest in the corner beside the window I took out my bridle carved with Spanish roses. I looped it over my left shoulder and eased myself back down the stairs. I felt my way through Glenisha's kitchen, which was softly lighted by the dying fire. In the rafters above the fireplace herring were hung to dry in golden rows, and from the wooden bins along the wall came the earthy smell of potatoes and carrots and onions that had been stored over the winter.

I let the heavy oak door close behind me. Outside, rows of old cabbages shimmered faintly in the kailyard and I turned past them to where, in silver and in shadow, were our cattle pens. It was there, in an empty one, that I'd bedded Sionnach for his first night in the Highlands.

I had not put my Spanish bridle on my new horse earlier, for I did not want a person like David Forbes to look on with a pair of prying spy's eyes. But it would be jolly, I thought as I hurried along, if Leofwin had been kept awake by the moonlight and decided to join me. I longed to talk to him as we used to talk. Among other things, I wanted to ask him why he had seemed less than happy to hear that our prince might come home.

Sionnach stood in the far corner of the pen, his breast-bone pressed urgently against the wood rails. His head was thrown high and he gazed out across the moor that we'd flown across only hours before. When he heard my foot-steps he whirled about, his bright coat almost black in the moonlight. He whinnied softly, lowered his head, and stepped toward me, shaking his long, silky mane as he came.

"I said you were bonny," I confessed to him, "but, oh, the word can't do you justice!" I took his slim, starry face in my hands, passed my fingers down his neck, down the swift slope of his shoulder, until I knelt in front of him with my hands clasped around each strong, deer-thin foreleg. He bent over me, and I felt his soft muzzle rest between my shoulder blades. "No brother ever gave a sister a finer gift than the one Leofwin gave me today!" I told Sionnach. I knew that Leofwin had chosen a bold red horse for me because he understood exactly the kind of girl I was.

As long as Leofwin had not come out to share the moon-light with me, I was quite content to be alone—so I was

28

vexed indeed to hear someone from the opposite side of the pen agree with me.

"Aye, he's a fine horse," came a voice that I recognized all too well. "There's no doubt he's worth many cabbage suppers!" I had hoped that Leofwin might join me; what I got instead was a certain pale-eyed person from Edinburgh.

"You're a stranger here, Mr. Forbes," I reminded him testily as I got to my feet. "It might not be safe for you to be out wandering about in the middle of the night."

"Or one of your father's clansmen might open my head with a Lochaber ax?" he teased in his clumsy way. The lad knows his Highland weapons, I thought. Carried into battle, a Lochaber ax could open an enemy's head, and it also had a hook on its side to snag a horseman off his mount. Taking Sionnach by the long, silky hair of his mane, I led him to the opposite fence where Mr. Forbes waited. The moonlight shone full in his face, and I studied Leofwin's friend peevishly from my side of the rails.

"Why did you really come to the Highlands?" I asked. I decided to confront him with what I knew to be the truth. "You've come to spy on Clan MacColl, haven't you, Mr. Forbes? No doubt you intend to carry wild tales about us back to the Privy Council. Perhaps you fancy seeing my father put to the horn again! Well, it's been tried before, Mr. Forbes, but no one can break a man like Big Archibald MacColl!"

David Forbes seemed genuinely taken aback. "I'm no spy," he protested. "Leofwin invited me to . . . that is, he wanted to repay my family for . . . I'm awfully sorry that you don't like me," he finished lamely.

If Mr. Forbes insisted on being decent, I thought, it was going to be hard to make him hate life in the Highlands. "It was quite wrong of you to make Leofwin doubt our prince," I scolded, eager to lay a burden of guilt on his shoulders.

"Prince Ch-Ch-Ch-Charles Stuart?" David Forbes stammered, "Oh, no, I'm sure I've said nothing that would . . . you see, Leofwin has a questioning mind, and he's gotten quite caught up in subjects like philosophy and history, which my father teaches. Such subjects encourage one to ask questions that have hard answers." He paused to draw a breath. "My father says that your brother is just the kind of new leader Scotland needs. In fact, everyone I know admires your brother."

"Everyone?" I asked suspiciously as I twisted Sionnach's red mane in my fingers. "Your sister, too, I suppose?"

David Forbes smiled agreeably. I was disappointed to see that his teeth were as white as Leofwin's. It would've been easier to find fault with him if they'd been snaggly and green-stained. "Elizabeth likes your brother well enough, I think," he replied. Well enough was too well to suit me. "It was she who plaited your horse's forelock and tied that green ribbon in it."

So . . . her name was Elizabeth . . . she could spare a pretty green ribbon to tie in a red horse's mane . . . and an hour ago my brother Leofwin had traced the letter *E* in Glenisha's tablecloth. I wanted to hear no more.

"You'd best go back to bed now, Mr. Forbes," I advised him. "Morning will be here before you know it, and you'll be obliged to be up and ready for the hunt." When he realized our conversation was over, he turned reluctantly and retreated up the stone path that led past the kailyard. I noticed from his footfalls that he wore heel-irons on his shoes to protect them from the wear of city streets.

I stripped the green ribbon from Sionnach's forelock and trampled it into the dirt. I slid the bridle off my shoulder and slipped its bit into his soft, willing mouth. I fitted the headstall over his ears, adjusted the browband, and fastened the throatlatch. I slipped three fingers between his nose bone and the noseband to make certain it was not too tight, then stood back three paces. In the silver light my stolen roses looked fresh enough to pluck.

"Now you are more a clever fox than ever," I whispered to Sionnach, "for you are all dressed up with roses that your mistress cobbed from a Lowlander and saved just for you!" I reached up to hang both arms around his neck.

His hide beneath my cheek was warm and smooth, and the night wind tangled his long mane with my own hair. I breathed deeply of the good, rich red smell of him. No cameos and no silk shirts for me! I thought proudly. No gifts that would make me feel soft and foolish or make me forget who I really was.

"And as soon as that spy is gone," I told Sionnach, "Leofwin and I can return to the life we used to live. We will have each other, and nothing else will matter." Leofwin would soon forget anyone whose name started with the letter *E*. The only thing that might make life even more perfect would be if Prince Charlie came home, too, and would take Scotland back for the Scots.

6

The morning was cold, and although the moon had been bright when I visited Sionnach at midnight, at dawn a heavy mist had rolled in off the waters of Loch Linnhe and trailed its ragged scarves across the moor. The forest to the south, which was our destination, was lost to our sight.

Leofwin called to Big Archibald's six deerhounds. "Aluinn! Creagan! Iolair!" Those three were our cleverest hunters and their names meant the fair one, the rocky one, and the eagle. My favorite was the fourth one, little Dorcha, the dark one, perhaps because she was as thin and lively as I was myself. Our two oldest hunters, Bras, who was so named because he was once the swiftest, and lame yellow Fiona could scarcely keep pace anymore with their younger companions.

David Forbes shivered in a coat that Leofwin had loaned to him and which was several sizes too large. He sat his knob-kneed horse with a pinched, unhappy look on his white face. "Perhaps you'd just as soon not ride with us today, Mr. Forbes?" I inquired sweetly.

He shifted in his saddle as if trying to find a suitable spot to rest his buttocks. "What I'd like best," he answered, "is if you'd please call me David. To be called Mr. Forbes makes me feel old and foolish and out of place." You're not old, I thought slyly, and smiled in spite of myself, but as for foolish and out of place, well. . . !

"Of course, *David*," I murmured agreeably. My change of spirit made Leofwin smile, and that was what I wanted. We three moved our horses out of the yard and headed south into the woods. The mist moved wetly against our cheeks, and I could feel the hair along my forehead spring into tight ringlets, as it always did when it was dampened.

Sionnach moved under me like an extension of my own person. I had to hold him back, for with his long, eager stride he quickly began to outdistance the lads on their smaller horses. Yet to be held back made my red fox impatient, and soon he was dancing sideways in the road again, his fiery head held high in the air. He chewed on his bit until foam flecked his mouth and began to spatter the leather buskins that covered my legs to the knee.

"No girl ever got a finer gift," I called over my shoulder to Leofwin. "How did you guess that I was wonderfully tired of riding just any old horse?" I asked. "How did you know that I wanted one of my very own?"

Leofwin cupped a palm around his mouth and called back to me, "Because you already had everything a wild child needs—a house with a blue slate roof, a good minnie, and six fine deerhounds!" Then he winked, turned to David Forbes, and continued just loud enough for me to hear: "But how she hates to lose races at the shielings! Three years ago, little Jamie MacKenzie finished three lengths ahead of her and she was cross for days!" It was true that I didn't like to be second best. I smoothed Sionnach's red neck and vowed that this year the outcome of the shieling races would be quite different.

Far ahead, their voices muffled by the mist, we could hear the dogs begin to bay. They'd caught the scent of a deer. In the headlong chase we'd soon have to give, I wondered if Mr. Forb—David, that is—might fall off his brown horse and damage his stiff Edinburgh dignity. Such a bruising might be the very thing to make him cut short his visit.

The dogs' cries rose to a wilder pitch and struck me as unusual. Perhaps they had flushed something extraordinary out of the forest. I reined Sionnach to a halt and the boys stopped, too. "Listen, Leofwin," I urged. "I think they've come on the track of something more than a deer."

Leofwin cocked an ear. Long before Leofwin and I were born, the forests around Ballachulish had been the home of wild boar and wolves, as well as foxes, badgers, and pine martens. Once, mountain lions even roamed the woods and were the reason the English still referred to us as the Lions of the North. The thick, golden pelts of such animals had adorned the garments of more than one clan chief, but not a single lion had been seen anywhere in the Highlands for more than 50 years.

"Maybe the dogs have fallen on a wolf," I suggested to Leofwin, for a den of wolves had recently been found in a corrie near Glencoe. "Wolf?" David Forbes echoed. "Perhaps we ought to turn back," he said, eager to do exactly that.

"Big Archibald sent us out to bring home venison for his

supper table, and Leofwin and I do not intend to disappoint him," I told David briskly and was pleased to see him flush with shame. Leofwin rode past me and set our pace through the mist in the direction of the hounds' voices. He knew there was no wisdom in plunging headlong toward we knew not what.

We found the dogs crowded around the base of a sheer black stone ledge. Young pines grew at its lower edge and the hounds thrashed back and forth among them, their eyes wild, their red tongues lolling. Fourteen feet above, from the rim of the ledge, a mountain lion stared down at us. Twin plumes of breath rose like smoke from its nostrils, and its eyes were the color of the topaz ring that Big Archibald had brought home from France and wore on his left hand.

"He's an easy target!" I cried above the dogs' mad howling. "Big Archibald will be a happy man when we bring home the hide of a Highland lion!" And just as clearly could I see myself wearing a coat trimmed with a bit of that dense golden fur. No one in all Ballachulish would be my match!

Leofwin looked up. When I remembered it later, it seemed that my brother and the gray-gold cat on the black stone ledge exchanged knowing glances. The lion's topaz gaze foretold the fate that awaited it only moments away. And Leofwin's—? His was a long, blue, thoughtful glance that puzzles me still.

"Take up your musket!" I urged him, for the lion presented itself to us full chest, its stout forelegs braced wide apart, and was a perfect target. A ball through its heart, I thought, and the whole length and breadth of that fine golden hide would hardly be damaged at all.

But Leofwin did nothing. He sat with his hands folded on the pommel of his saddle. "No," he said at last, his voice deep and mellow, "that old fellow might be the last of his kind in these hills. It would make me happier, Haddie, to know he was free, a lord in his own realm, than for any of us to wear his pelt on our backs."

I stared hard at my brother. A peculiar coolness closed itself around my heart. It was a chilliness that had nothing to do with the mist in the woods or the fact that it was only April. Three years in Edinburgh have made him different, I finally admitted to myself. Leofwin had gotten soft. *Soft!* It was the fault of David Forbes and foolish men like his father, of that I was certain. They'd filled Leofwin's head with nonsense that would never be of any use to him in the Highlands. To live in the high country, one had to be hard.

What Leofwin needed, I decided—maybe David Forbes, too—was to have that fact pointed out to them.

I raised my musket, loaded it quickly, tamped down the charge, and let it go. The roar of the shot collided with the hillsides around us. The lion on its ledge stood fast, even as a wound opened over its heart and blossomed on its golden breast like a great red rose. Its amber eyes fixed me with a look of recognition, as if to say, *Ah, only you—only you, Hadder MacColl—could have done this deed!* A moment later the cat went down without a sound and seemed to melt into its own tracks.

"What a trophy to carry back to Big Archibald!" I declared, pleased with my shot. "He'll boast of this to anyone who'll listen. I wouldn't be surprised if word of this catch travels as far as Edinburgh!"

With my eyes I dared either one of the lads to say otherwise, but I was not prepared for the expression that came
across Leofwin's face. He turned to stare at me as if we were
strangers, and although I had never dreamed of such a thing,
I knew suddenly that we were.

"Aye, it was a handsome kill!" Big Archibald agreed
heartily when we got home. "Leofwin let you have the
first shot and you didn't miss, eh, lassie?" he teased. I did
not explain that if it'd been Leofwin's choice the lion would
still be on its black throne in the forest, and the lads kept
their tongues quiet as well.

"We'll have the tanner make a collar for your coat,
Hadder," my father promised, "and a purse to wear about
your waist." I might not have been the daughter my mother
had dreamed of, but Big Archibald was always pleased when
I was as headstrong as he was himself. The lion was not our
only catch, however; Leofwin had brought down a red deer,
and we feasted in silence on the roasted haunch that
Glenisha fixed for our supper.

Afterward, when the house was as quiet as it'd been the
night before, I crept out of bed again. This time I did not
go to visit Sionnach. Instead, I stole down the hall past the
room where David Forbes slept, then up a narrow flight of
stairs to the only room at the top of the tower. I wanted to
explain to Leofwin that three years away from the Highlands had made him forget how hard we all had to be.

An edge of light shone from beneath his door, and I was
glad that I would not have to wake him. When I stepped
into the room, it was to see that Leofwin had lighted a

candle at his bedside and was reading. He laid his book across his knees and welcomed me with a smile. I had been so afraid he might never smile at me again!

"I'm sorry that I made you unhappy today," I said quickly, anxious to get my apology over with, "but perhaps you have forgotten that we of the clans cannot afford to be soft or sentimental."

"Ah, Haddie," Leofwin sighed, "it was as natural for you to raise that musket to your shoulder as it would've been for Big Archibald to do the same if he'd been there himself!" As Leofwin spoke, I saw no bitterness in his eyes. "The two of you are so straight and fierce, Had. You allow for no compromises! You are far more our father's child, lass, than I have ever been."

"That isn't so!" I objected loudly. "It's we two who are—" Leofwin quieted me with a finger held to his lips, and I lowered my voice. "*We* are the ones who are alike, Leofwin," I insisted. "You said so yourself the day we made our pledge. And after you've been home a while longer, you'll be just the same as you used to be!"

A shadowy look crossed Leofwin's face, and once again I noticed the hollows beneath his cheekbones. "You mean that I will be as eager as ever to lift cattle from our neighbors or to cob their books and newspapers as I used to be?" He shook his head. In the candlelight his hair was as shiny as brass and curled sweetly behind his ears.

"Haddie, what you suspect is true," he warned me as he ran a finger slowly down the spine of the book he'd been reading. "I *have* changed, lass. I'm not the same Leofwin I used to be."

Without waiting for an invitation, I climbed onto the end of his bed, the better to argue with him and keep my feet warm at the same time. "But you always liked the way we lived, reiving and thieving and all that," I reminded him. "Why, nobody laughed louder than you did when Black John came home with that rose-colored window on the back of his horse! Father says we of the clans have lived this way for four hundred years, and I hope we live this way forever!"

Leofwin sighed and tapped my knee with his finger. "Our mother should've named you Forever MacColl," he said ruefully, "for that has always been your favorite word!" Then he frowned, as if debating with himself about something else he wanted to tell me. "Socrates has changed my mind about forever, Haddie," he said after a pause. "That word doesn't mean the same thing to me that it used to."

"I never heard of such a person," I objected. "How could a stranger change your mind about something as important as forever?"

Leofwin held up to me the book he'd been reading and I spelled out the name on its green leather cover: S-o-c-r-a-t-e-s. "Socrates was a philosopher who lived in Greece hundreds of years ago, Haddie," Leofwin explained patiently, "and he said that an unexamined life is not worth living. So when I think now about the life we Highlanders live, quarreling and stealing and carrying our grudges to our graves, I am not as pleased with it as I used to be." He hesitated, and when he raised his eyes to mine they were bright with purpose.

"You know what I'd like to do, lass? I'd like to go off to

39

the colonies of America and start my life afresh and forget the kind of history we Scots let ourselves get trapped in!"

I jumped off his bed, glad that the floor under my feet was cold enough to remind me of where I was and who I was. "What you need," I told Leofwin slowly, "is a whole summer spent at the shielings. That will sweep the cobwebs out of your head! For what can a man who lived in Greece hundreds of years ago know about our life in the Highlands?" I answered my own question. "Nothing! But when summer is over and when that David Forbes has gone home, then you'll be glad you are a descendant of Coll, and you won't think about the colonies anymore!"

But when I was in my own bed, as the house made its small night sounds around me, I thought about what that Socrates person had said: an unexamined life is not worth living. Well. Maybe what Leofwin needed even more than a summer at the shielings was another trip into the Forest of Forever. But to take him there with David Forbes always hanging about would not be easy to manage. Sweet, dark little Dorcha had crept upstairs and into my bed while I had been visiting Leofwin, and when I finally went to sleep with my feet pressed against her warm ribs, I dreamed that Mr. Forbes had left us for good.

Two weeks later, a letter came to Ballachulish. "For Master Leofwin MacColl," said the man who'd helped to carry it all the way from Edinburgh. I took the letter myself, since both Leofwin and David Forbes had gone off to help Big Archibald load a cart for the journey to the shielings that would begin in the morning.

40

The handwriting on the envelope was pretty and precise. I held the letter up to my nose and sniffed. It smelled of lavender talcum. Its long journey had left it dog-eared, and one corner had been torn loose enough for me to see the ivory-colored paper inside. Pressed into the red sealing wax on the back of it was the letter *E*. I folded the letter in half and put it in my pocket. Glenisha watched me with a narrow eye and wagged a finger under my nose.

"Cheelie, you are bent on doing something spiteful," she scolded. Glenisha liked to think she knew me very well.

"Not in the least," I informed her airily. "I will give Leofwin his letter as soon as he gets back." And I fully intended to—just as soon as I had a chance to read it myself.

7

My father's humblies, his common folk, had assembled themselves, and their wagons were loaded for the journey. A few families had already begun the trip to the shielings and were strung along the road, singing like tinkers on their way to a fair. Their children ran beside the wagons, happy to be free as bees for the summer. Threaded through it all was the skirl and skriegh of the bagpipes.

Big Archibald had two pipers, and the father of Jamie MacKenzie, my old adversary, was one of them. Each piper had a bagpipe made of sheepskin sewn with thread that was thicker than the needle, so that the bag would be airtight when it was finished. The reeds of the pipes were made from cane, and the chanter and bass and tenor drones were made of cocuswood that was imported from the West Indies. Yards of silk ribbon in the colors of our clan, yellow and blue, trailed from each.

Our brown cattle, more than six hundred strong, moved slowly across the heather, and the bulls tossed their heavy, long-horned heads at anyone who dared come too close to the cows with their new yellow calves. "What's it like, this place we're going to?" David Forbes wanted to know when Leofwin was drawn away from us by a commotion at the head of the moving train of humblies.

I felt almost sorry for him. David Forbes had never spent a summer at a shieling! "You'll have a finer time than any in your life," I assured him grandly, "for we live life on the loose in the summer, just like the wind. Our women spin— not inside their cottages, but right out in the open air. They make cheeses, too, and gather berries for jam. In the afternoons we often have races, and this year it'll be Jamie MacKenzie who chews dust, not me! Almost every night we have a ceilidh, a gathering around a fire, when stories about the old times are told."

I remembered my real mission too late: I was supposed to make David Forbes hate shieling life, not love it! "But the cottages themselves are such common things," I hastened to add. "Their roofs are made of turf and their walls are dry-set stones, which means that beetles and mice wander in and out as they please—sometimes right across your face at night when you're trying to sleep! I'm sure it will all be quite different from the tidy life you're used to living in Edinburgh."

David Forbes smiled, and I wondered if he recognized in my words my wish to send him packing as quickly as possible. "It makes you happy, doesn't it, to enjoy another summer like all the ones that've gone before?" he murmured.

"And like all the ones that shall come after," I declared. The word *forever* turned slowly like a golden wheel inside my head, tarnished only slightly by the conversation I'd had with Leofwin about Socrates. I still had no wish to examine my life; to live it day by day was quite enough for me. Just the same, I added pointedly: "Leofwin told me all about that man named Socrates. My brother and I share everything, you see."

David Forbes nodded. "My father said Leofwin was the finest philosophy student he'd ever had. My sister thinks our father and your brother are cut from the same bolt of cloth." It was not news I was glad to get, but since the subject of David's sister had been raised, I decided to pursue it.

"What's she like?" I inquired idly, as if the answer to my question was not especially important. "Let me see, I can't quite remember her name." I pulled on my ear as if the answer might fall out if I tugged long enough. "Edith? Ermintrude?" I knew perfectly well it was Elizabeth. It was David himself who'd told me so the moonlit night we faced each other over the bars of Sionnach's pen.

"Elizabeth, and she's not much like you," David said, then hastened to explain. "What I mean is, my sister doesn't know how to ride a horse or fish or shoot lions." He pursed his lips as if trying hard to remember what she *was* like. "Elizabeth does lovely needlework, though, and she paints, too." Ah, this was the sort of girl my mother would've loved!

"Truth to tell," David went on to boast, "Elizabeth paints very well. She takes lessons three times a week and she's even done a portrait of your brother. It's very small; I think she meant it for a locket," he told me and measured a space in the air between us that was about the size of a plover's egg. And does she also mean to wear it on a ribbon around her neck? I wanted to ask but kept my tongue still, for I was quite sure that I did not want to know the answer.

A moment later there was no time to worry about the matter, for Leofwin came riding toward us so hard that Sionnach leaped sideways and nearly left me flat on my backside in the middle of the road. "Come quickly, Haddie," Leofwin called to me. "One of the children has been hurt, and Glenisha is calling for you to come and help her." I pounded my heels into Sionnach's red sides, glad to escape any further mention of that girl who painted pictures the size of a plover's egg.

It was Ada who'd been hurt; she had been run over by the wheel of one of the heavy carts. She was only four or so, the daughter of a humblie named Rollie Simpson, who brought fresh-killed rabbits and grouse to Big Archibald in exchange for a small patch of land near Ballachulish. Ada lay on the ground, her mouth open in a wide *O*, her eyes black as currants with pain. The wheel had passed over her leg, a puny limb no bigger than a kindling twig, and the bone poked whitely through her torn flesh.

"She ought to have stayed closer to her mother's side," Big Archibald growled from nearby. "The journey to the shielings can't be stopped for every cheelie who has an accident."

My father was accustomed to wielding the power of pit and gallows over his humblies and tacksmen, but his words sounded harsh and uncaring to me because I knew that Leofwin was at my side and heard them, too. "It wasn't her fault," I said. "She was only playing and having a fine time. It might've happened to anyone."

Big Archibald fixed me with a black look. "Back on your

horse, lass," he commanded as I began to dismount. "The cattle need tending. You, too, Leofwin. On your way now, both of you. Let the child's mother and Glenisha do whatever needs to be done."

Ada's mother, a thin woman aged before her time, cradled the child's head in her lap while Leofwin and my father locked glances. My brother's eyes, pale blue in the bright light of morning, were calm and unperturbed. "I'll have to take Ada to Fort William," he said quietly. That fort, built by the English and staffed with soldiers who were supposed to keep peace in the Highlands, was many miles away. "There will be a surgeon there," Leofwin explained, "who might be able to help the child. For now, you'll all have to go on without me."

"No such thing!" Big Archibald thundered. "We need no help from the English! We'll take care of our own! But if this child's time has come, then it's come. For the rest of us it's shieling time, my lad, and you'll muster the herd along, as is your duty!"

A light wind lifted Leofwin's yellow hair off the nape of his neck. A bright spot appeared on each of his cheeks. He held out a pair of long, strong arms to Glenisha. "Lift the child up, minnie," he ordered. "We'll hurry; she won't last long if we don't."

"It's a devilish long ride to the fort," Big Archibald observed sourly. "The cheelie will be gone hours before you ever get there." Leofwin only smiled, folded Ada Simpson against his breast, and rode back along the road we'd just traveled over. Ada Simpson's mother ran weeping behind, wringing her hands, her kerchief askew.

46

My father sat his horse and watched them disappear, then turned his eyes to the sky and studied the flight of a golden eagle that coasted on the air drafts over our heads. "The lad is—oh, he's different than he used to be," he mused to no one in particular. When David Forbes rode up, all out of breath, Big Archibald announced gruffly, "You'll have to take Leofwin's place for the time being, Mr. Forbes, even though you are a poor excuse for a Highland-man! But that child won't last long. Leofwin will be back with us before the sun goes down tonight."

What my father said was true: in the high country, a wound such as the one Ada Simpson had suffered usually meant that death came quickly. But now that I knew a person was supposed to examine life, Big Archibald's words clamored harshly in my ears. I had longed for Leofwin to come home but now that he was back with his books and his peculiar ideas, nothing sounded the same or looked the same to me anymore.

The small stone cottages that we called shielings were scattered hither and thither across Rannoch moor. They smelled musty when we moved into them each year, for rats and mice had lived in them all winter. Glenisha's first task each springtime was to make a broom out of heather and sweep ours until it was spotless. I usually found something else to do until all the cleaning was done but since I wanted to avoid the company of David Forbes, I stepped in to help.

"Don't trouble yourself, cheelie," Glenisha said, her voice bright with surprise. "I can do this just as I've always done

47

it. Besides, you have your fine red horse to ride, and if you want to beat Jamie MacKenzie you ought to be practicing to do exactly that!"

Just the same, I made a broom for myself and set about housecleaning. "It will go faster with two of us," I told her. By afternoon, the corners of the cottage were clean, and we'd laid a carpet of fresh heather over the stamped-earth floor. Glenisha started the supper fire in a circle of stones just beyond the doorway and soon had a pot of stew boiling. Alone at last, I sat in a corner of the shieling as the late afternoon sun spilled across my knees and drew Elizabeth Forbes' letter from my pocket.

I stuck my little finger carefully in the torn corner of the envelope and pried up the flap. It lifted easily, and I began to read with greedy eyes. "My dear Leofwin," she began in her delicate script, shaping the *e* and *o* of his name with special care. He is not *your* dear Leofwin! I wanted to inform her crisply, then read on:

"How I shall miss you this whole endless summer! I will mark the days until you are back in Edinburgh and we can speak once again of your plans to go to the colonies." I raised my glance from the page and stared across the moor. Out there, Sionnach grazed with the cattle, his coat as bright as flame against their shaggy brown ones. Leofwin had never planned to stay with us in the Highlands . . . he dreamed only of the colonies and of a girl who might join him there. And that girl was not me. I read on, chilled in spite of the warm sunshine that spilled everywhere.

"Your company has been dearer to me than I can tell you," Elizabeth Forbes continued. "Am I too bold if I confess that I have pressed between the pages of my favorite book the flowers that you gathered for me on my birthday? I examine them every day, and think only of you.

Most sinc'ly,
Elizabeth F."

So. I folded the letter and put it back in my pocket. So. My mouth was dry. My heart felt pinched. I was almost glad when a shadow fell across my sunny corner and I looked up to see David Forbes. His presence meant that I would not, for a moment at least, have to think about the words I'd just read.

"You were quite right," he informed me with a smile. "This will be the finest holiday I've ever had!" His forehead was sunburned, for he had helped Glenisha and me gather heather to carpet the floor of the shieling. He didn't look like a ferret anymore, much less a spy, which was a trifle annoying.

"Then it's a pity you won't be staying with us longer," I observed. He seemed amazed to discover that he'd be leaving so soon. I explained his departure to him: "It's hard work, you see, helping to birth the cows that are calving late, moving the cattle around the moor every day, all that sort of thing. And the weather can never be counted on to help. It's either hot and dusty or it's rainy and muddy, neither of which you'd care for for a whole summer, I'm sure." My voice was brisk and confident, for I knew it had to be. If I could manage to get rid of David Forbes, I could eventually find a way to get rid of his sister, too.

David Forbes knelt at my side, his hands clasped between his knees. "I really wish you liked me better," he lamented.

"You're Leofwin's friend," I reminded him, just in case he'd forgotten.

"That doesn't mean I can't be yours, too," he pointed out. "After all, Leofwin and Elizabeth are—"

"Kindly do not gossip to me about your sister and my brother," I exclaimed. "Besides, I need only one friend at a time, and right now Leofwin is the only one that I want." I was determined to shut out of my mind the suspicion that Leofwin might want something quite different for himself.

Glenisha stirred the pot in front of her, then filled two plain brown pottery bowls with stew and held them out to us. David Forbes and I ate our meal in silence. We had just finished our second bowls when Leofwin came riding slowly toward us across the heather. The sun had already set, but the sky was still rosy and the reflected light on my brother's face transformed it into a mask sculpted in metal. Except for his eyes, that is, which in the fading light were two transparent blue windows through which shone an other-wordly glow.

David rose up quickly. "How is the child?" he asked before I could ask myself. Leofwin looked down at David and hesitated before he replied. "My father was right," he admitted softly. "Ada was too frail to stand the journey. We'd gone only a few miles before. . . ." His voice trailed off. Then he laid his palms across Birkie's neck and slid off the pony's back with one long, smooth, easy motion. "So we made a place for the child in the heather, Ada's mother and I, and we built a cairn of stones above her. It was hard; you see, Ada was the Simpsons' only child, and her mother will not likely bear another."

David Forbes nodded and the silence that he shared with Leofwin closed me out. But I knew one way to intrude upon them. I reached into my pocket and took out the letter addressed to Leofwin. I had taken care to press the red sealing wax back in place.

"This came yesterday when you were packing the wagon," I explained matter-of-factly, with no show of remorse over the fate of Ada Simpson. For although we had a stranger in our midst and little Ada was gone and a letter written on ivory-colored paper had come for Leofwin all the way from Edinburgh—in spite of all those things—I knew that I could find a way to make my life right again if only I was strong and did not weaken.

And happily, when Big Archibald returned to the shielings six weeks later from a trip he'd had to make home to Ballachulish, he came with news that I was sure would help me. On July twenty-third, during a hard rainstorm, Prince Charles Edward Stuart had landed with seven companions on the island of Eriskay.

Eriskay is three miles long from north to south and only half that distance across. It is but one of about 200 tiny islands that float like green gems from a princess's necklace on the blue-gray waters of the sea next to the coast of Scotland. The names of those islands, like that of Eriskay itself, have always been music to my ears—Mull and Skye and Tiree and Jura—and of course Coll, where Big Archibald's father and grandfather were buried.

It might be thought that we called our prince by the name Charlie in the same way an Englishman might use the diminutive of the name Charles. The truth is that in Gaelic our prince's name is Tearlach, the *Te* being spoken as *Ch*, the whole of it being spoken as Charlie. As soon as Prince Charlie landed, he issued a call for a gathering of the loyal clans. They were asked to meet on the nineteenth of August at Glenfinnan, where the hills folded down, blue and brown, on either side of Loch Shiel.

"Mark me, now things will begin to happen!" Big Archibald exulted when he repeated the news to MacDonald of

Sleat, who had camped overnight with us on his way home to his own hills. "I'll set a cross to blazing this very night to call all my tacksmen," my father declared. "I have a hundred that I can count on right away, and more when the need arises."

Leofwin seemed bemused by our father's high heart. "I will look after things here at the shielings until you return," he promised, with a smile that made him look older than his years.

"You'll be at my side, that's where you'll be," Big Archibald corrected my brother at once, his black eyes narrow and fierce. "It's my only son, after all, that I want riding with me when we meet the prince of the house of Stuart!" He frowned, and with a broody look took David Forbes into account. David stood well outside of the circle that had included Leofwin and me and MacDonald of Sleat, who was one of my mother's kinsmen, a man well over six feet tall with a face as blunt as a hammer.

"It's your friend we'll be leaving behind, Leofwin," my father said. "Since he's here for the summer, he can earn his keep by helping Hadder tend to shieling life in our absence. You and I have bigger matters to look after!" Which plainly meant that *I* would not be meeting the prince at Glenfinnan.

I hid my disappointment as well as I could. "How long will you be gone?" I wanted to know. First of all, Leofwin had scarcely come home and now he was going to leave again. Second, David Forbes was not my notion of splendid company while I waited for Leofwin to return. "No doubt we'll be back within a week," Big Archibald assured me.

"The prince will want to lay battle plans; then we'll ride home quickly in order to gear up for the war that is sure to be ours."

As soon as MacDonald of Sleat had ridden off and David Forbes was out of earshot, I offered Leofwin a chance to present himself to the prince in a manner that would assure that his highness would not soon forget the name MacColl. It was the way I'd have presented myself if I'd been lucky enough to go along, too.

"Ride Sionnach to Glenfinnan," I urged Leofwin. The spectacle of my brother with his golden hair loose on the wind, mounted on my tall red horse, made it almost easy for me to let both of them go. "The prince will always remember Clan MacColl if you do," I promised him, "and who knows, when victory comes, the prince might see fit to deed us a good stand of timber! Or maybe a few more acres along Loch Linnhe!"

"Haddie, Sionnach is your horse, not mine." Leofwin sighed. He still did not seem the least bit thrilled by the prospect of a new Stuart rising. "In a way, the red fox belongs to both of us," I persisted, for that is what I believed. Leofwin and I were of one blood, in spite of the fact he pretended it didn't matter anymore. "You gave Sionnach to me and I accepted and he was all paid for with all those cabbage suppers you had to eat!" I tried to tease him, just as David Forbes had teased me. But the shadow behind my brother's eyes would not be erased.

"Oh, whatever is the matter with you?" I exclaimed so loudly that Big Archibald, who sat his horse some distance away, turned and looked on curiously. "You are more of an old woman than Glenisha has ever been," I ranted. "Once upon a time, you were quicker than anybody for a tussle or a raid! But since you've been to Edinburgh, Leofwin, nothing seems to please you anymore!"

Certain phrases that I was not supposed to know anything about came back to haunt me. My dear Leofwin . . . your company has been dearer to me than I can tell . . . the flowers you gathered for me on my birthday. . . . Well, having memories like that had made Leofwin witless. Worse, they'd robbed him of his old Highland courage.

"Ah, Haddie," Leofwin sighed, his lips curling in a smile while his eyes remained somber, "David was right—you *are* a willful, vauntie lass!" He turned in his saddle so that he faced me straight on and fastened me with his blue eyes, now melancholy. "Don't you realize what the prince's landing means? He's come home to win the crown for his father and to name himself as regent. It means rebellion; it means war. *War*, Haddie! Not just more poetic talk around a ceilidh fire, but the terrible misery of war."

I couldn't believe my ears. Why, Leofwin sounded like a lad who wore lace jabots at his throat and slept on silk sheets! "You've gotten as soft and silly as a girl," I chided him. And I knew who was to blame, too: it was that miminy-piminy, pale-necked thing who wrote him letters perfumed with lavender.

"*She's* the one who's done all this to you!" I declared, too bitter to realize the secret I was about to give away. "'Your company is dearer to me than I can tell you,'" I mimicked in a thin, fleeching voice. "'I have pressed between the pages of my favorite book the flowers that you gathered for me on my birthday.'"

Leofwin stared at me with horror. "The only way you

could say those words, Mary Hadder MacColl, is if you'd read my letter from Elizabeth Forbes. Did you open it before you gave it to me?"

"What if I did?" I snapped, not the least bit repentant. "Anyway, we used to share everything. Now you keep secrets to yourself. And I can't understand why you'd want to leave the moors and mountains and forests of the Highlands to go to the colonies of America!" I emphasized the word forests and hoped Leofwin would remember the Forest of Forever. But he only continued to stare at me in disbelief, which inspired me to press him harder.

"I suppose you even call her Betty," I snickered. "Betty-Letty-Setty," I raved on in a smirky voice that I hardly recognized, "who powders her nose and puts curlpapers in her hair every night and couldn't ride a horse if you threw her on one and—"

"Stop, Haddie," Leofwin interrupted. "I think you might like Elizabeth if you ever met her." Oh, it was hateful of him to be so reasonable when I was so outrageous! "And to answer your question—no, I don't call her Betty or Letty or Setty. I call her Elizabeth because that is her name, and I think it is a pretty one. She makes me think of—well, Haddie, she makes me think of our mother."

"Our mother?" I echoed blankly. It was my turn to stare in horror. Our mother, golden-haired and gentle, was the one Leofwin remembered whenever he thought of Elizabeth Forbes? My heart felt like a trapped bird in the cage of my ribs, for I realized perfectly well what it meant. Leofwin loved Elizabeth Forbes just as much as she loved him.

"I wouldn't let you ride Sionnach tomorrow even if you

56

begged to," I hissed at him. "But remember this: we mingled our blood and made a pact to be true to Clan MacColl. If you are honorable you will live up to that pact, just as I would live up to it myself!" I galloped after Big Archibald. It was plain that I would have to shame Leofwin into supporting the prince and his cause. So be it. But when the rebellion was over and we'd all come home with booty of cattle and horses—maybe even with gold and silver and fresh stands of timber—why, Leofwin would realize I was right and would be glad I had been strong when he'd been weak.

David Forbes and I watched them go, my father's banner of blue and gold streaming brightly in the summer wind, the raised pikes of his humblies showing like a spiky black hedge against the sky, until at last the thin, wild cry of the bagpipes was lost to our ears. "How I wish I could've gone myself!" I groaned, then was sorry, for it seemed the same as treason not to be glad to do as Big Archibald had bidden.

To my amazement, David Forbes agreed. "Aye, it would be fine to meet the last prince of the house of Stuart. I would treasure such a memory myself." For weeks, I had persisted in regarding him as David Forbes, ferret and spy, but a rare thing had overtaken him as the summer days had passed. His skin had burned and peeled and burned again until now his face was the good, honest color of polished walnut and his scorched hair covered his head like a cap of ripe hay. Worse than that, his mild gray eyes often studied me with glances that were suspiciously sweet and affectionate.

"It's time to get the cattle out," I muttered hastily, which made him sigh and shrug. "Take them out, bring them back! Why not just turn them loose and let them graze where they please?" he wanted to know.

"Because someone from another clan might take a notion to lift a few, that's why," I answered crossly.

"But you're all Highlanders," David Forbes objected. "Why do you go around stealing from one another?"

"Because that's what we've always done!" I snapped. "Cattle-lifting isn't exactly the terrible crime you Lowlanders fancy it is. It's a way of proving power, and as Big Archibald says, he'd rather have a strong neighbor than a weak one. Anyway, we've lived this way forever and ever."

"Forever may be a dangerous word, Hadder," he murmured softly. When he said my name like that it sounded formal and serious, as if he was as old as Leofwin, and I knew he was two years younger, for Leofwin had told me so. "Of course it isn't dangerous," I corrected him, "and nobody knows that better than Leofwin. After all, it was my brother himself who named that place in the forest where we made our pledge." I realized, too late, that I was once again confessing too much. Unhappily, my words had already captured David Forbes' imagination.

"What did Leofwin name it, that place where you made your pledge?"

"The Forest of Forever," I answered vaguely.

"I would like to go there sometime," he ventured.

"Oh, it's much too far away," I assured him quickly. "Besides, it is important only to Leofwin and me." I toyed carelessly with the long red strands of Sionnach's mane. He bent his head and began to graze as the cattle lifted themselves one by one from the heather where they'd rested all night like dark boulders against the earth. I inspected the horizon carefully in order to avoid David Forbes' glance. It would be at least a week before I saw a brave blue-and-gold banner flying there, but although I was already lonely and he was eager to be my friend, I continued to protect my glance from that of Mr. Forbes.

Glenisha packed biscuits for us and wrapped a smoked herring in a linen cloth. "Be back before nightfall," she cautioned me after I put Rollie Simpson, one of the humblies who'd been left behind, in charge of the cattle. Then David Forbes and I turned west to ride along the road we'd traveled from Ballachulish so many weeks before.

The sun was past its zenith before we came to the place at the edge of the woods where the narrow path was hidden. I was always able to remember exactly where to turn, however, by the presence of the clean, white skeleton of a dead birch tree only a few feet from the path itself. I motioned David Forbes to follow, and he rode silently behind me on the trail that led us deep into the woods.

The pines grew so thick all around us that they screened out the sun, and the light inside the forest was as mellow as that of evening time. While the wind always seemed to blow across the moor, no leaf swayed in the woods through which we traveled. It was Sionnach's first time on the trail, too, and he lifted each hoof carefully, his head up, his nerves tightly tuned.

When we arrived at the black pool, David Forbes and I

stopped to stare at our reflections. "This is the place Leofwin decided we should call the Forest of Forever," I said, speaking more to myself than to David Forbes, for I still did not know why I had let him accompany me. "It was here, on this very spot, that we pricked our fingers with a dirk and promised always to be true to each other and to Clan MacColl. And now—"

"And now Leofwin doesn't believe in forever anymore," David finished for me. Before I could take offense at those words, he gestured toward the dark water, the gnarled trees that surrounded us, the violets that bloomed in the shadows and went on to admit, "But a place like this invites a person to believe that forever *is* possible." He turned an agreeable glance on me. "Now that I've been here, I think I understand you better."

"No, you don't," I admonished him, "and you don't really understand Leofwin, either." I kept my own glance on the edge of the pool where I knew kelpies were hiding and listening to our every word. "Because you're not a Highlander, that's why," I explained. "You have to have been born here, you see, and be raised up as close to the earth as grass and trees and water." I paused. "Only then can you understand what it means to love the Highlands—and to be ready to die for the Highlands."

9

Seven days later, my father and Leofwin and our humblies returned to the shielings. They fetched back booty, too—three fine dark cows and their yellow followers. "They invited themselves along," Big Archibald joshed, pleased not only by his acquisition but by the fact they'd been lifted off a tacksman from Clan Campbell. Big Archibald had never forgotten that it was the Campbells who'd fallen on my mother's people and was pleased to take even the smallest revenge on them. As Leofwin said, we carried our grudges to our graves—and often beyond.

Around the ceilidh fire that night, my father told of his meeting with the prince. He leaned close and touched his wide shoulder to mine as he spoke. "You'd have admired him, lass," he confided to me with a gleam in his black eyes, and his next words invited me to see exactly what he and Leofwin had witnessed.

"Dressed like a regular civilian, our prince was, and wore a vest of lemon yellow," he began. "There was a scarlet cockade in his bonnet, and when he unfurled the Stuart banner—it was crimson, my girl, with a spot in its center of

61

purest white—his manner was cool and full of purpose. Just then, Cameron of Lochiel came over the hill with his piper and seven hundred of his clan, and the laird of Moray rode down with a hundred and fifty! Gordon of Glenbucket arrived with almost a hundred and we MacColls had seventy-five—why, we'll all be sworded and shielded and on our way across the border into England in no time!"

A moment later, however, Big Archibald recalled something that displeased him. He pounded his knee angrily. "But when the prince called for pledges from the clans, not a man spoke up until I did myself! 'I'll lay down my life for you, and so will my bonny son!' I told him, and a light rose up in the prince's eyes at my words. He put a hand on my shoulder," my father reported, and he touched his right shoulder as if he still felt the weight of five royal fingers there, "and said to me, 'I knew I could count on my brave Highlanders, sir!' "

Leofwin, whose life had just been promised, said nothing at all. He stared into the fire and smiled a quirky little smile that turned up the corners of his mouth but never brightened his eyes. "What did *you* think?" I pressed him. "Was the prince just as grand as Father claims?"

"Aye, he's every inch a prince, Haddie, that much cannot be denied," Leofwin admitted. "But it's plain that not all of the clans are in favor of another rebellion. They remember too well the punishment that followed the Rising of the Nineteen—all the hangings and floggings and all the men who were broken by the horn." Leofwin laid his chin on his knee and when he continued, I knew his words were meant as much for Big Archibald as for me.

"The men in Edinburgh and London live in fear of our

lawless ways, and if the prince succeeds in raising the clans again, the grayheads will panic. They will seek to crush us any way they can, and will give us no quarter." My brother poked at the fire with a stick while David Forbes listened, too, his eyes as grave as Leofwin's.

"Someone even fetched a copy of the *London Gazette* to Glenfinnan," Leofwin went on. "In it, there was an offer of thirty thousand pounds sterling for the prince's capture! And it is rumored that King George will appoint his own son, the Duke of Cumberland, to put down the rebellion if it comes. Which means," he added with his odd, melancholy smile, "that there'll be three lads on the battlefield who want to honor their fathers—Prince Charlie, the Duke, and Leofwin MacColl!"

Big Archibald was greatly pleased by the association. "As it should be," he growled complacently. "One day it will be Prince Charlie who takes his father's place on the throne of Britain, and you will one day ride at the head of Clan MacColl. Aye, as it should be!"

That morning, David Forbes and I had shot a half-dozen fat grouse, and Glenisha roasted them in the evening after rubbing them first with wild rosemary and thyme and stuffing them with barley. Big Archibald devoured a whole one all by himself and smacked his lips many times before he finally wiped his face on the sleeve of his coat. He'd long ago forgotten the foxy gloss to his manners he'd acquired in France when he was young. Then he studied David Forbes with a look of regret.

"Your friend will have to take himself home to his own folk," my father sighed, turning his glance to Leofwin. He spoke with a gentleness that surprised me. Perhaps he was remembering the friends of his own youth and the fine times they had shared. War was war, however, and now he addressed himself to that. "We shall soon be too busy getting ready to ride with the prince to need the distraction of strangers in our midst," he explained, resting his back against the stone wall of the shieling. With his chin on his chest, he began to doze and to dream no doubt of a lively war that would deliver Scotland to the Scots. Without a word of protest, David Forbes crept away from the fire and laid himself on his bed of heather inside the cottage.

Leofwin watched him go with a haunted look. "It will be a fine war," I assured him, hoping to take that look out of his eyes. In the light of the fire the dark hollows of Leofwin's cheeks were deep enough to hide chestnuts in. He sighed and massaged his eyes with the heels of his hands.

"No, Haddie, it won't be a fine war at all," he chastened me. "It will be a desperate and bloody one, just as most wars are. Somehow, Had, we Scots have to learn to live with the English on this little island we call Britain. We have battled each other for centuries, at Sheriffmuir and Inverlochy and Glenshiel. We've laid too many lads to sleep under the heather! It all must have a stop. We must look for better solutions to our troubles with our old enemies."

"You could always run off to the colonies if you're afraid to fight," I suggested and was astonished that I wanted to hurt him, to punish him. "That's what cowards do, you know; they run away!"

"Haddie, I'm no more a coward than you are," Leofwin replied wearily.

"Just the same, I wish we could trade places," I told him bitterly, "for it's plain your heart is not set for battle and

64

mine is! You want compromises—and I want victory! You talk about examining life—but I am ready to lay mine down for the Highlands!" I scrambled away from my place by the fireside and left him alone there. I settled myself beside Glenisha, and when she felt my warmth, she eased her sharp, old-woman's bones close to mine.

I made a pillow out of my bent arm, and when I looked through a crack in the stone wall, I could see that Leofwin had pulled Elizabeth Forbes' letter from his pocket and was reading it again. He's soft and foolish and a stranger to me, I realized. So be it. I would not be a stranger to myself. I closed my heart against Leofwin and wondered if a girl had ever gone to war before or if I might be the very first one.

When morning came, it brought with it the moment I had schemed and dreamed about since I first laid eyes on David Forbes, but it was not quite as sweet as I'd always imagined it would be. It was harder to say good-bye to Leofwin's friend than it ought to have been.

David Forbes managed a shy farewell to Big Archibald, who did not care a whit if he got one or not. Then he muttered a kindly one to Glenisha, who was glad for any attention he paid her. All the while, I kept my back turned. Just be gone, be gone! I thought impatiently. When he realized I did not intend to be sentimental but merely to wave him away, David Forbes finally mounted his old brown horse. I watched him go down the road with Leofwin, who wanted to share a few private moments with his friend.

The two dismounted a quarter-mile away. They faced each other, Leofwin taller by a head than his friend, and to my astonishment, they embraced each and exchanged kisses on one another's cheeks before David got back on his knob-kneed horse and continued alone on the road that twisted south across the moor.

"Good riddance," I told Leofwin coldly as soon as he came back. The look he gave me in reply was the same kind Glenisha gave me when I was rude. He seemed to think he was years and years older than I was instead of only four. "Haddie, I want you to ride after David and say a proper farewell to him. I don't want to remember that even in parting you insisted on being rude and disagreeable to him."

"What difference can it make—" I started to object warmly, stung by Leofwin's words.

"Because David's a decent lad who never meant you any harm," Leofwin interrupted. His glance softened and he took a strand of my hair between his thumb and forefinger. "Don't be afraid to like him, Haddie. It's time for you to grow up and learn to care for someone other than me. It's time for you to be more like other girls."

I threw myself furiously onto Sionnach's red back and galloped down the road after David Forbes. More like other girls . . . never! Yes, I would say good-bye to David Forbes if it would help ease the differences between Leofwin and me, but not because I ever wanted to change. David Forbes turned in his saddle when he heard the clatter of hoofbeats behind him and the sight of me made a smile light up his narrow, burnished face.

"Leofwin thought I ought to tell you a proper good-bye," I informed him so that he would understand the idea was not my own.

"I'm glad," David Forbes answered, and the honesty in

his voice grated on my nerves. "I didn't want to travel all the way home to Edinburgh without thanking you for showing me how to gather cattle in the evening, for taking me to the Forest of Forever, for things like that which I will never forget."

"At least your days at the shielings have put a bit of color in your face," I observed grimly. "You were pale as a bogle when you got here; now you look a bit like a real Highlander." When silence fell between us as thick as fog, David Forbes fumbled in his pocket and drew out a piece of paper. "I w-w-want to give you my address, Hadder," he stammered. I waved his hand away, for the notion of writing to him made me feel old, grown up, not like myself at all. Or was that how Leofwin wanted me to feel? "Like other girls," he'd said, as if that suddenly was important.

"Oh, I'm quite sure that I will never have cause to—" I began, but David Forbes pressed the square of paper into my hand before I could object any further. "No one can foresee how the prince's plans will turn out," he went on, "and sometime you might well have cause to write to me, or perhaps even to come to Edinburgh someday."

I closed the paper in my fist and wheeled Sionnach smartly about. "I have been rude and testy and disagreeable to you," I fumed. "You know full well that I have never welcomed your presence here, nor have I been soft and sweet and jolly as girls are supposed to be! Why have you persisted in being decent?"

"Because underneath it all you are not as hard and remorseless as you think you are, Hadder MacColl," David Forbes informed me. His boldness made his cheeks turn pink.

"And you are vain enough to think you know me better than I know myself!" I retorted. "Well, you don't at all!"

"Nevertheless, I will think of you often," he insisted. "And maybe you will think of me, too."

"I might," I lied, for I had no intention of doing any such thing. David Forbes lifted one brown hand in a wave, and I waved briskly back. When he'd gone several paces down the road, I inspected the piece of paper he'd left in my hand. *David M. Forbes*, it read, *Northbridge Road, Edinburgh*. I looked after him; he was growing steadily smaller and smaller in the blazing August distance.

I crumpled the paper and let the wind hide it in the blooming heather. Never in the world would I have need of David Forbes' address! I leaned forward until I was stretched the length of Sionnach's neck. "He's gone at last, my fine fox, gone at last!" I whispered. "Now it will be just Leofwin and me, just as it always used to be!" But as Sionnach and I flew across the heather to where Leofwin waited for us, that fact did not fill up my heart with the same kind of happiness it once had.

Big Archibald put Jamie MacKenzie's father in charge of life at the shielings and picked his other piper, Alexander Gillespie, to accompany him on the journey back to Ballachulish. Prince Charlie had already traveled on to Loch Eil and on August twenty-third had marched with John Cameron to within a few miles of Fort William, where he camped well out of range of the fort's cannon.

"Let me ride to Ballachulish with you," I begged Big Archibald. If I managed to get that far, maybe I could find a way to get to war, too. "I will help you pack oats and barley and meat for your men, and I promise I will not get in the way or cause you any trouble!" I promised. "Please, oh, please!"

It must have been exactly the kind of opening Leofwin had been waiting for, for it was then that he announced his own plans. "No harm will be done by letting Haddie travel as far as Ballachulish," he spoke up, "and she can return with me to the shielings when you and the men are gone." He paused while Big Archibald and I turned to him with amazement. "You see, I'll be coming back here to the shielings," Leofwin continued, "for I do not intend to follow Prince Charlie into his war."

At Leofwin's words, a scarlet flush stained Big Archibald's neck like spilled elderberry wine. "We have had this kind of conversation before, laddie," my father observed in a low and dangerous voice. "You *will* go with me, and I will hear no more about you staying behind. What you need is a good taste of battle to clear your head of some of the foolish ideas that have lately been put into it." Big Archibald, like me, was sure that he knew what was best for Leofwin.

I saw two familiar tight, white lines appear around Leofwin's mouth. "No, Father, I won't be going," he insisted in a voice just as low and forbidding as my father's had been. Big Archibald whirled his garron about, and the stout little horse, jarred by the anger in those two voices, laid its ears back as flat as a weasel's to its neat little head.

Big Archibald tucked his heels hard into the pony's belly, and when the horse skittered nervously, my father continued to jerk on its reins to control it. The pony squatted on its haunches, for it was not accustomed to being treated so badly, then it reared in the air and pawed the sky in alarm. Big Archibald struggled to keep his seat, but his balance was gone and he came crashing down into the heather. The shriek that my father raised to the sky then was not one of anger but one of horrible pain.

Leofwin and I jumped off our horses and hurried to his side. Big Archibald's leg was twisted outward in a most unnatural way, and Leofwin quickly tore off my father's buskin.

Big Archibald's leg was thick as a tree trunk, and I would've thought it could never break. Nevertheless, a stout white bone stuck through the flesh that was covered with curly red hair, just as a tiny white twig had poked through Ada Simpson's skinny leg. Yet rather than cry out again in anguish when Leofwin leaned over him, my father seized my brother hard by the arm.

"Our clan has been pledged to follow the prince, and you were pledged, too," I heard him grate at Leofwin through clenched teeth. My father's black eyes were knife-thin slits of mingled pain and rage. "*I* cannot lead the clan now—but *you* will!" he hissed.

The gaze Leofwin turned on my father was clear and blue and quiet. Was he thinking of what it truly meant to be the son of a clan chief? I wondered. Leofwin, being a boy, knew far better than I that when a chief's son came to manhood, he was watched by all the folk of the clan. If he was quick to take revenge for any dishonor, if he was nimble when it came to cattle-lifting, if he was eager for a tussle, then he was much admired and brought credit to his father's name. If he was none of those things, he brought embarrassment to the whole clan.

"Aye, I will do it," Leofwin answered so softly I could barely hear his words. Then I understood. While he thought nothing of shaming himself, of becoming soft and foolish and harboring silly ideas, he could not bring himself to dishonor our father.

Big Archibald pulled his lips back from his great white teeth in a grimace that was made of equal parts of pain and satisfaction. I might have smiled myself except for a peculiar vision that entered my head the moment I heard Leofwin say, "Aye, I will do it." It was the image of a lion on a black cliff in a forest, a lion whose clear topaz gaze seemed to foretell the fate it knew awaited it.

10

Leofwin's first letter, which he had written in September, finally arrived in Ballachulish at Christmastime. I needed no other gift to make my holiday perfect. My brother's handwriting went straight up and down on the page rather than slantwise, and I imagined him beside a fire in some field far away, taking special pains to write to me. I tried to avoid any suspicion about letters he might be writing to someone else.

"Greetings to my dear, fierce Haddie," he began. Although he could not say "I forgive you," that is what I heard him tell me as I read his letter aloud to Big Archibald.

"On the 3rd of this month we traveled through the Pass of Killiecrankie while Cameron of Lochiel led a band of men forward to occupy the city of Perth," Leofwin wrote. "Your Pr. looked grand as he entered the city that evening, lass, riding on a gray horse loaned to him by MacDonald of Tirnadrish and wearing a handsome suit of tartan trimmed with gold lace. Your Pr. is a tall man, Haddie, has a small but lively eye, and need not wear a wig as is the current fashion, for he has a full head of light-colored hair. He has made his headquarters at the Salutation Inn in High Street, and already has received the Duke of Perth and Lord William Drummond."

Your prince, Leofwin had taken care to point out to me, but I suspected he'd been impressed himself. I read on, greedy to share everything he'd been lucky enough to witness.

"The Pr. attended church in Perth this morning and I went, too. The minister was a chap named Armstrong, and in a fine, steady voice he gave us a sermon taken from Isaiah, 14:1–2—'For the Lord will have pity on Jacob . . . and will make captives of those who took them captive, and rule over those who were their masters.' The rebels call themselves Jacobites, which means followers of James, for that is the name of the Pr.'s father, so the sermon had special meaning for Pr. Charlie. I could see a light rise up in the Pr.'s eye, Haddie, at Mr. Armstrong's choice of scripture.

"On Sept. 11th, but two days hence, we shall press on for Stirling, where the English have sent Sir Johnnie Cope to await us. I will ride in the first detachment of troops. So you see, lass, your brother has not been a coward nor has he brought any dishonor to Clan MacColl. But every night, Haddie, I lay myself close to the back of my good little Birkie so that both of us may be warm, and I study the starnies overhead. Out of this confrontation, Haddie, I hope that I can learn some wisdom that later I might put to good use.

Yr. Bro.,
L. MacC."

How clearly could I see Leofwin in that field, studying the stars whose light was so cool and came from so far away—and how I longed to be there, too! As things were, Leofwin would end up with all the wisdom and the honor, and I would have nothing at all to show how much I believed in the rebellion.

I folded Leofwin's letter into a tidy square while Big Archibald shifted his great weight on the narrow cot he'd lain on since Leofwin marched away at the head of Clan MacColl.

The cot had been carried down from one of the rooms above, for my father could no longer struggle up the stairs. Every morning Glenisha washed the ugly wound in Big Archibald's leg with salt water or vinegar, but instead of healing nicely and closing itself over the bone that had been set while my father let out bloodcurdling screams, his wound kept festering and oozed an odorous yellow matter.

"The man needs a doctor," Glenisha told me. When Big Archibald overheard her words he thumped on the wall beside his cot with his fist until his knuckles were raw.

"I'll heal in my own time, old woman!" he bellowed. Rather than dwell on his wound, Big Archibald much preferred to speculate on the courage and spirit of the son he'd sent to war. "The lad sounds like a true MacColl again," he confided to me, but sometimes I suspected the glitter in my father's black eyes owed itself more to fever than to fervor. I noticed that his thick brows were often beaded with pearls of sweat, and once when I straightened his pillow I was astonished to see that his fiery mane was suddenly bestreaked with gray.

As the winds of January probed the cracks around the doors of the White Tower and as he hoped his leg would soon begin to heal, Big Archibald and I continued to measure our lives by the letters we got from Leofwin. My father was usually content to hear them only once, but I read each one until it was worn quite thin.

"We panicked our enemies at Colt Bridge," Leofwin wrote in a letter that came to us in February but which had been written many weeks earlier. "Three of us surprised a whole battalion of Englishmen on the bridge over the Water of Leith while we were on patrol. Without waiting to see that we were only three in number, the enemy fled with a clatter of hooves across the bridge. The next day, the English claimed it was an orderly withdrawal—but we call it the Colt Bridge Canter! Tomorrow we shall be camped near Gray's Mill, which is only two miles southwest of Edinburgh."

"And then into the city itself!" Big Archibald exulted, but his voice had lost all its old timbre and nearly every day there was a bright spot of color on each of his cheeks. "Fetch me a map, lass," he instructed one afternoon, "that same map I used to teach you your history lessons when Leofwin was gone to school."

When I took the map from its place in the trunk that also held Barbara MacDonald's wedding clothes, my father told me to take up a pen and mark the route of the Highland Army, beginning with the raising of the standard at Glenfinnan. Fassifern, Achnacarry, Corriearrick Pass, Bannockburn, and Linlithgow—oh, how the names of such places filled up my heart! I came too soon to Edinburgh.

Edinburgh. My skin prickled and grew cool. That place meant only one thing to me: it was where pale, proud Elizabeth Forbes lived. David Forbes lived there, too, of course, but I had almost forgotten even what he looked like. Besides, *he* was not the one who caused me grief; it was the awful suspicion that Leofwin would sneak away from his men to visit David's sister. But Leofwin's very next letter erased all my fears.

"To the lass who believes in forever," Leofwin hailed me, and I knew he hadn't forgotten a single word of the pledge we'd made so long ago.

"Today at Mercat Crossing in Edinburgh, the Pr. proclaimed his father James as the rightful king of all Scotland and England. We then rode on to Holyrood House, at the end of the Royal Mile, and the park was full of well-wishers. The Pr. wore traditional Highland dress, Haddie—a short coat of tartan, a blue bonnet on his light hair—and the Cross of St. Andrew hung from a green ribbon in his lapel.

"As we were all about to enter the palace, silver-haired James Hepburn of Keith (tell Father this old gentleman hates the Union as much as he does himself!) held his sword aloft and strode up the stairs before the Pr. The crowd cheered, for James Hepburn is as full of courage as he is of years, and the Pr. clearly took the gesture as a good omen."

But I took care not to read aloud to Big Archibald the postscript that Leofwin had added to his letter.

"P.S. As I passed through King's Park behind the Pr., a mother snatched her child close to her side and whispered loudly in its ear: 'Mind yourself, for wild Highlanders such as him will eat a child like you!' Ah, the poor little wight; she was no bigger than Ada Simpson and will carry with her forever the idea that a Highlander might have boiled her and eaten her for supper! What is it about human hearts, Haddie, that ascribes such dreadful wickedness to those whom we do not even know?"

I had no answer for Leofwin. As David Forbes had warned me, hard questions don't have easy answers.

There was one letter, however, that Big Archibald asked me to read to him three times. It was the one Leofwin wrote after the Battle of Prestonpans, and it recounted the kind of furious clash my father liked to dream about.

"At daybreak," Leofwin wrote, "Sir Johnnie Cope mistook for bushes what was in fact our front line, positioned about two hundred paces in front of his army. We had twelve hundred men in that line, and six hundred more in our second line. For lack of better weapons, our clansmen took up scythes, sharpened them well, and attached them to the ends of sticks that were six or seven feet long. We dealt sword strokes with such weapons to the noses of our enemies' horses, for such blows made the horses bolt in pain and threw the squadron into terrible disorder. It was a cruel and ugly thing to have to do, but I did it along with the others."

I shuddered each time I read those words, for I could think only of Sionnach or Birkie taking such a blow.

"We lost no more than three or four officers," Leofwin went on, "but Sir Johnnie C. had three hundred killed and we took eighty of his officers as prisoners. The Pr. ordered that the enemy wounded should be cared for and sent carriages to take them from the field. I was nearby when the Pr. gave those orders and noticed that his boots and knees were muddy. He seemed to have fallen in a ditch. I was told later that he had! He fights and suffers like any commoner, Haddie."

When Leofwin's next letter came in March, he had news that made Big Archibald scowl and grind his teeth with outrage. "The Frasers have come out for our cause," Leofwin told us, "but MacDonald of Sleat and MacLeod of the Isles have gone over to the Gov't. side. The MacKenzies, the MacIntoshes, the Gordons, and the Grants are all divided in their allegiance. One of the agonies of this rebellion, Haddie, is that it has separated father from son, brother from brother, neighbor from neighbor. Up north, even the MacKays and the Sutherlands and Monroes have gone over to the King. But Cluny MacPherson has come over to us, so now we can count five thousand Foot and five hundred Horse. We are headed now for Inverness and truth to tell, I wish we had more Horse!"

"They need more Horse," my father muttered, his face gleaming with sweat in spite of the coolness of the room, "and I lie here as worthless as a broken stag!" For even as we read Leofwin's letter, Big Archibald's leg still had not healed. One morning as Glenisha prepared to wash it she noticed that thin, fiery lines radiated from the wound like a sunburst. She took me quickly aside.

"The infection is running for his heart," she whispered behind her hand. "And when it reaches here—" she paused and thumped her own heart emphatically, "then it will be all over. Your father should go to Oban. A port city like that is bound to have a doctor. I am just an old woman who only knows how to treat cheelies with skinned knees or dogs that've been chewed by lions. *I* cannot save him."

Big Archibald was white and shivery and too weary to object when we carried him out to the cart that waited in the snowy yard. His companions of old wouldn't have recognized their Archibald of the Strong Blows, for the hand that gripped mine as we parted that morning was thin-fingered, and veins stood out on it like the blue lines I'd used to trace the path of the Highland army on our map.

"Victory will be ours before I have a chance to raise my claymore!" he tried to joke, but his voice was only a hoarse whisper and the flesh on his neck, which once had been taut and ruddy, now hung loose like dewlaps on an old bull. "Look after things, lass," he bid me as the cart hauled out of the yard. I waved after him, but he was too feeble to lift his hand in reply.

Soon it was April and snow remained only in scattered patches on the moor. I took myself to the pens, where Sionnach reared up to welcome me with a high, imperious whinny. I knew he loathed our idleness even more than I did. He pressed his breast hard against the wood rails of the pen and blew his hot, sweet breath on my cheek. I laid my face against his slim red one but stepped back, ashamed to be so sentimental, when Jamie MacKenzie came around the corner of the pen, carrying a young lamb in his arms.

"All summer long you were afraid to race me," he teased with a sly wink, "and I'll wager you're not ready now either!" Jamie MacKenzie's hair was as thick as the pelt of a pine marten, and his eyes were as black as my own. He seemed taller than I remembered him to be, and his shoulders were no longer thin and sloping like a child's but were broad as a man's. I took my Spanish bridle off my own shoulder and shook it under his nose.

"Aye, more than ready, Jamie MacKenzie—if you fancy being second, that is!" I threw back at him. Everyone said Jamie MacKenzie was a lad who'd break many hearts, and although I knew he'd never break mine, his charm made it impossible to stay angry with him for long. Besides, since nearly everyone else had gone away to war, Jamie and I now shared a common fate: we were the ones who'd been left behind.

The horse Jamie MacKenzie rode was not an ordinary garron but had some Lowland blood in it, which gave it longer legs and a coat that was dark brown instead of dun. Yet it had the wide, deep chest of a garron and a thick, bowed neck like its Highland ancestors and would be hard even for Sionnach to outrun. As soon as Jamie had put the lamb to suck with its mother, however, we headed together for the moor east of the White Tower.

"If only I'd been older I would've gone off to war with all the others," Jamie informed me. "I hate it, staying behind with the old men—and the girls." He gave me one of those bold looks that all the girls in Ballachulish loved so well but which did not impress me overmuch. When the moor stretched before us, bleak and empty and spotted with snow, Jamie MacKenzie turned to mock me again.

"Are you ready?" he asked me softly, and his glance measured me in a way that let me know he was eager to speak of other things as soon as our race was finished.

A cold wind swept off the mountains of Glencoe and punished our hands and faces. The water of the loch was glassy, with ice at its edges. "I'll race you to that boulder on the left," I told him coolly. He nodded, and we hunched side by side, high over the withers of our horses.

A moment later we were both leaning into the wind, and the snow underfoot, mixed with the tiny, dried brown bells of last summer's heather flew up from the pounding hooves of our mounts. I tucked my knees close to the points of my elbows and stretched my forearms along Sionnach's neck so that my weight was far forward. But Jamie on his lean, dark horse had an edge on me. I loosened Sionnach's reins until I exerted only the slightest pressure on the bit, and let him have his head.

"You can't be second-best, because your heart is just like mine!" I cried into his laid-back ears. At those words, Sionnach flattened himself over the heather and began to shorten the distance between his nose and the dark, flying tail of Jamie MacKenzie's horse.

I was so intent on erasing the distance between our mounts that I saw the ditch in front of us when it was too late to turn aside. Jamie had time to take a swerving course, but if I'd asked Sionnach to do the same, he might've gone down and smashed both front legs. The ditch, which had been carved by melting snow water, opened like a yawn beneath me, and in the next instant Sionnach launched himself into the air above it.

I hung onto Sionnach's back like a burr, knees up, elbows tucked in, head low, too startled to close my eyes. The gallant red fox arched over the ditch as sure as an arrow let loose from a bow and came down on the opposite side in one long, smooth, effortless motion. As soon as he landed, he gathered his hind legs beneath his body and shot past Jamie, who'd come the long way around.

I looked back over my shoulder. Jamie's dark eyes were round with amazement as the distance between our mounts widened. The pounding hooves of our horses scattered the dry heather bells like grapeshot in the snow, and I turned my face back into the wind, glad for the harsh sting of Sionnach's red mane in my face. For one wild moment I was sure I could hear the sound of pipes . . . that I could see the blue-and-gold blaze of the MacColl banner on the horizon . . . that I was riding into London at Leofwin's side!

I raised my clenched fist into the air. "I am strong and not afraid to die, and will pull my thunder from the sky!" I cried, and I turned to wait for Jamie MacKenzie to catch up to me. It was then, as I uttered the *pibroch* that my clan had used for four hundred years, that I knew what I had to do.

Glenisha and I ate cold, sliced mutton for our supper and drank two pots of dark tea. "The house seems empty without your father's grumbling," Glenisha murmured as we watched our shadows flicker on the wall. It was true, of course; Big Archibald, even when he'd been thin and ill, had seemed to fill up the house with his presence. In his absence, everything around us seemed to have shrunk and lost its bold color.

Glenisha carved scraps of mutton fat off her meat and

fed them to Aluinn and Creagan and Iolair. Dorcha and yellow Fiona came around to my side of the table hoping for tidbits, but old Bras slept on, dreaming his old-dog dreams beside the fire. "Pray that it will all soon be over," Glenisha advised me. She always said *it* when speaking of the rebellion. "Pray the lads will all soon be safe at home."

"Of course they'll come safely back," I told her. How could it be otherwise? Leofwin was too brave and bonny ever to die. But Glenisha wagged her head at me, and her cotton-grass hair was so fine that I could see her smooth, pink scalp beneath.

Only old people die, I thought, but was not cruel enough to say such words to her. Leofwin, on the other hand, was young and golden and walked with a step as springy as a stag in the forest. Nothing would ever happen to Leofwin.

In my bed that night, as the fire winked at me from the grate, I repeated out loud the names I'd culled from Leofwin's letters that seemed to have a ring of destiny about them: "Colt Bridge . . . Gray's Mill . . . Prestonpans. . . ." I hugged myself and felt my own bones through my thin chemise. Long, strong bones they were, full of strength and courage.

"We are headed for Inverness and I wish we had more Horse," Leofwin had written. I studied the dying fire with sleepy eyes. I wished that I could lead a hundred mounted men with hearts as hard as my own to fight by Leofwin's side, but there was only one person I knew I could count on. Tomorrow, that person would do what needed to be done.

"What are you up to, cheelie?" Glenisha asked warily. She pulled her kerchief more snugly about her head and watched me as I loaded oatmeal and cheese and two loaves of barley bread into a sack.

"I'm going," I told her.

"When?" she inquired softly. Wise, good old Glenisha! She didn't ask where, for she already knew. She didn't lecture me or tell me that girls did not do such things, nor did she ask me to stay behind, for she knew it would be the same as asking a bird to shut its wings.

"If the weather holds, I'll leave after breakfast," I told her. "I've thought about it for a long time," I explained, "but it was too cold in December and it seemed important to stay because of Big Archibald. But now. . . ." I let my sentence finish itself.

Just the same, my decision meant that Glenisha would be left alone in a house big enough to billet a small army. I touched her lightly on the arm. "Thank you for not telling me to stay," I murmured.

"A muckle of good that would do!" she retorted

spunkily. She rolled her hands into her apron so that they were covered as with a muff. "Of course, I don't fancy being left all alone, one old woman to manage all of this." She gestured with her wrapped fists at the house around us. I peeked at her from the tail of my eye.

"Now, Glenisha," I cautioned, "do you think I've forgotten what you did to that tinker who came to the door when I was five? The one who tried to steal your tartan cape?" She had scalded the poor fool with a pot of hot barley water and was the talk of Ballachulish for weeks! "I think you will be quite all right. And I will be home before you know it. Why, I'm sure our prince has the Whigs' backs to the wall this very moment, and they must be nearly ready to surrender."

"I expect you'll be riding your fine red horse," Glenisha observed with a frown. "You'd be better off, you know, to ride away on a common pony," she went on. "Sionnach is a horse who calls attention to himself and would be a prize for anyone. You are only a girl and might have a hard time fighting for him."

I drew my dirk out of the small scabbard that was strapped below my knee. "I am a girl who knows how to take care of herself," I reminded her. Still, Glenisha was not satisfied. "If I were you," she murmured, "I'd give that red horse a nice mud bath. I would make him look so knock-kneed and ugly that no one would look twice at him." It was a clever idea; after all, Big Archibald regularly reived from those who were not alert, and there was no doubt someone along the way would try to steal Sionnach from me.

Glenisha finished packing for me while I hurried to the pens with a pail of warm water. Along the way, I scooped up soil from the cabbage patch. While Sionnach looked on, I stirred it all into a thick paste. Next I rubbed it all over his fine, slim legs, even adding a bit of straw here and there. Rather than brush out his mane and tail, I stuck straw and burrs into them so that they hung down, clotted and coarse.

I stepped back three paces to survey the animal I had invented. Sionnach was so chagrined by his new appearance that he hung his head, which further improved his image as a broken-down old cart horse. No one would want such a creature; he looked as if he would never live to see another spring. Sionnach's lowered head was even with the clasp on my belt, and I hugged him hard against my belly.

"Don't feel ugly," I whispered, "because of course you could never be, any more than Leofwin could! Your heart is just as bright and brave as it ever was, but I must keep you safe. As soon as we find the prince and Leofwin, I'll clean you up, and you'll be as bonny as ever."

When I returned to the house, Glenisha had finished the packing and had only one request of me. "Leave in the morning, cheelie," she begged. "Stay with me one more night, then go with my blessing." It was a small thing to ask, and for supper she cooked long pudding for me and stuffed a salmon with herbs and barley. We sat, just we two, at Big Archibald's great oak table and dined like royalty. The candle-light cast flickering shadows on the white walls, and on the hearth I could still see the dark stain where I'd thrown a piece of venison so long ago. "Send me to Edinburgh!" I had challenged my father that night, for I had never wanted to be separated from Leofwin. In a few days I would be with my brother again, would share the adven-

86

tures of the rebellion with him. Afterward, we'd be together forever.

Before I mounted Sionnach the next morning, I tied my hair into a knot and pulled one of Leofwin's old wool caps over my head. There was no reason for me to look like a girl as I set out. I took one of Big Archibald's heavy tartans, the one he'd worn over his shoulder and fastened with a silver clasp at his waist, and tied it behind my saddle. Like a clansman on a journey, I could roll up in it to sleep or could spread it over tree limbs to make a kind of tent. Lastly, I shrugged myself into my coat that was trimmed with lion's fur.

All the dogs except old Bras crowded around Sionnach's feet as I mounted, thinking we were off on another good hunt. "Lock them away," I told Glenisha, "for if they follow me they'll create such a racket as will raise the dead." She beckoned them into the great hall, then returned to say good-bye. I looked down into her eyes that were sweet and mild as a child's, and she laid a small, withery hand on my knee. I didn't cover her fingers with my own, for I knew tears would sting my eyes if I dared such a gesture.

"Don't forget that yellow cow who was bred early will soon be calving," I told her sternly. "And I will write to you," I promised, which made her smile.

"But I cannot read, cheelie," she reminded me, which made both of us laugh. Then I was off and down the road. I only looked back once. Glenisha stood by the gate and behind her, the house that belonged to the children of Coll and that always was a surprise to my heart loomed softly white and tall in the thin April sunshine.

For the first time, I saw not only its loveliness but wondered: *will* it last forever? I waved merrily to Glenisha to banish the sudden suspicion that it might not and hoped that as I rode away I looked as much like a lad as Leofwin himself. Glenisha, small as a doll in the distance, raised a doll's frail arm to me in farewell. Then I put my heels into Sionnach's ribs and he broke into a gallop. I was off to war at last.

On our first night away from Ballachulish, Sionnach and I slept in a thin grove of alder trees beside a loch whose name I did not know. I grazed the red fox until it was dark and when he laid himself down in the dry grass, I rolled myself into my father's tartan and settled myself against Sionnach's broad backside. He breathed softly as the night deepened, but I wished that I had fetched dark little Dorcha with me for extra company, for to my surprise, I was already homesick!

"You're a fool, Hadder MacColl," I scolded myself. Sionnach stirred sleepily at my words. "Soldiers who go to battle don't carry their pets along to keep them company," I reminded myself, and only then did I drift off to sleep.

In the morning, the bleak moor to the north was still shrouded in mist. I put Sionnach on a long tether to let him graze while I built a small fire with alder twigs and heated water for tea. I broke off a piece of barley bread and tried to calculate how long my two loaves would last. Two or three days, I decided, but by then I would surely have caught up with the prince and his army. It would be fine to see him, that royal person with a small but lively eye, as

Leofwin had described him. Most of all, though, it would be jolly to be with Leofwin again.

And when Leofwin saw me—? He would turn on me his wide, white lion's smile, and his eyes would be clear and blue and happy, for he would know that I, too, had been true to our pledge. "Ah, my little toe-rag," he'd say in his low, rich voice, "my vauntie sister who sticks like a burr to the back of any horse she rides!"

I studied the blue line Big Archibald and I had drawn on our map. It started at Glenfinnan, where nine months before the prince's standard had been raised. Glenfinnan lay to the northwest, at the head of Loch Shiel, in a narrow valley flanked by mountains on either side, between which the River Finnan flowed. "When the Pr. moved east," Leofwin had reported, "he had to bury twelve large swivel guns and some small cannon at Loch Eil because he didn't have enough Horse to pull them along." I wondered if I dared go to Loch Eil and try to rescue a cannon. Even a small one might help. I gave up the notion, however, and proceeded to Ft. William.

I passed the fort on the north side of the River Lochy, just as the prince had done, and stayed safely out of range of the English cannons. I traveled northeast along the river, and before I mounted the bridge that crossed the River Spean, I read a plaque that informed me:

In the ninth year of His Majesty, King George II, this bridge was erected under the care of Lt. General Wade, 1736.

I sniffed. Soon there wouldn't be an Englishman left to build a bridge anywhere in Scotland!

Sionnach and I traveled mostly at early morning and in the evening so that his outrageous color (which the mud did little to conceal) would not be noticed by other travelers. In such dim light I was also much more likely to pass for a lad than a lass. Between dawn and dusk, we kept ourselves hidden in small patches of woods or in corries.

At Invergarry, a woman gave me oat cakes and cold boiled potatoes along with news I hadn't heard before. "There were many desertions from the Highland Army after Edinburgh," she lamented. "Some clansmen thought the war had gone on too long and were anxious to get home to their wives and bairns before winter settled on them." When I got to Invermoriston, a girl not much older than I was myself passed a meal of cabbage and leeks to me through the back door of her parents' cottage.

"Did you hear the prince got as far as Swarkstone Bridge, but had to turn back? Only a hundred and twenty-seven miles from Londontown—what a pity!"

"Have you seen the army yourself?" I asked her, wondering if by chance she might've seen Leofwin. She pouted and hooked a finger in the corner of her mouth. "I went to Edinburgh while the Highlanders were camped there, but they moved on before I could find myself a likely fellow!" I decided not to mention that I was looking for my brother.

After the cabbage meal in Invermoriston, I had only tea to drink for two days, and to still my hunger, I had to eat a handful of dried berries that had clung all winter to some vines in a woods where Sionnach and I slept one night.

When I was five days away from Ballachulish, I still had not seen the prince or his army. On the sixth day, from a hilltop where I had camped, I could look over a wide meadow. The wind came at me from the opposite side, bending the grassheads and tree crowns as it came, and I held out my arms to catch it. "We'll find them soon, soon," I promised Sionnach.

But that night it rained. The sky opened in a wrathful way and water poured down in sheets and I shivered miserably under Big Archibald's wet, heavy tartan. No doubt Leofwin had been cold and wet at some time during his march with the prince, so I whispered to myself, "Endure, endure!" When I shared the experience later with Leofwin, it would only bring us closer.

On the seventh day, having caught a fine brown trout where it was trapped in the shallows of a narrow loch after the tide went out, I feasted and felt refreshed. As I licked my fingers clean, I studied Sionnach. The mud I'd daubed on him had been nearly all washed off by the rain. What he needed was a good brushing, I decided. I had no brush, of course, but I gathered some dry heather into a bundle to fashion a brush of sorts, and with it I smoothed his red coat until it shone.

"Your disguise did you no permanent harm," I assured him. It would be only another day or two until we found Leofwin, so I was no longer concerned with covering up Sionnach's fine appearance. "There," I told him when I stepped back to appreciate his glossy good looks, "you are as handsome as ever!"

"Indeed he is," came a gruff voice from the trees near

which we'd camped. I whirled about to see a stranger coming toward me out of the shadows of the woods. "Are you far from home, laddie?" the man inquired slyly, and he eyed me in a way that made my heart jump. At least he mistakes me for a boy, I told myself.

I hesitated a moment before I answered, for I knew I ought to reply in a boy's low voice. "Not far," I lied hoarsely. "I come from just over the hill." A shrewd, unbelieving glance persisted in the stranger's eyes and made the hair on my neck prickle with alarm. "My father is one of Big Archibald MacColl's tacksmen," I lied again.

"One of the tacksmen who stayed at home," the stranger pressed, "or one of those who rode off to war?"

"My father lost a leg in the Rising of the Nineteen," I murmured, "so he stayed behind to look after things until the prince puts a run to the Englishmen."

"The prince has picked a big bone to chew on," the stranger mused, his eyes small and bright as a squirrel's. "Cameron of Lochiel himself tried to talk the lad out of such a mad rebellion. The prince is headed for Inverness now—hoping, no doubt, to find French boats in the harbor that will carry him back to France where he belongs!"

"I, for one, am glad that he came!" I declared, stung by the stranger's lack of faith. I bent and pretended to pluck a burr from Sionnach's fetlock; what I really meant to do was pull my dirk from its scabbard at my knee. As I did so, my cap fell off and my hair came tumbling down. I snatched up the cap and stood up to find the stranger as startled as I was myself.

"Aye, I thought I knew ye!" he exclaimed. "You're no

lad and you're not an ordinary tacksman's daughter either! You're Big Archibald's own bairn and ought to be worth a fine ransom! I'll do him a favor and keep you safe until he comes home and can pay royally to get you back. . . ."

The stranger reached for me with a hand that was as greasy and gray as a sheep hide that'd lain under the sun all summer. I stepped nimbly aside and bumped into Sionnach's wide shoulder. "Not likely," I told my would-be captor, but fear made my voice squeaky. Sionnach eased himself between us and gave me the chance I needed. I grabbed a handful of red mane and pulled myself onto the red fox's back.

The stranger seized hold of my heel, only to have Sionnach wheel around and, with bared teeth, catch him by the arm. The kidnapper's coat shredded like straw in the grip of those long, yellow teeth, and with an oath he let me go. I pounded my heels into Sionnach's sides, and he lifted us both over the grasstops as the stranger rained curses on our heads.

"We abuse our friends just as readily as we persecute our enemies," Leofwin had told me once. At the time, his words had meant nothing to me. But a moment ago, a fellow Highlander had wanted to hold me for ransom, might even have slain me if he hadn't got the sum he thought I was worth. "We are a wild, fierce folk whose time is running out," Leofwin had warned me. Had he been more right than wrong, after all?

I counted up the days. It must be almost April fourteenth, I concluded; I'd been gone from Ballachulish for eight days.

It meant that nearly a year had passed since Leofwin came home, yet in all that time I'd seen him for only a few weeks. But when I went through Drumnadrochit, a lad came along the road leading three goats and told me that the Highlanders had gathered at Culloden Moor, about twenty miles away. That meant Leofwin and I would soon be reunited.

"My father says it is a bad field to pick for a battle," the lad told me. "Highlandmen fight best on rough ground, so what's the sense of choosing a battlefield that's as flat as a tabletop?" I could see the boy was only ten or so and paid little attention to his opinion.

By evening time I still had not overtaken the Highland army and had to camp one final time by myself. I staked Sionnach where there was plenty to eat and had three eggs for myself that I'd cobbed from a henhouse near Inverness. I wrapped them in wet oak leaves and laid them to bake in the hot coals of a fire, for I'd lost my cooking pot to the stranger in the woods.

I ate my eggs slowly and reflected on the news the lad with the goats had passed on to me. The Highlanders were gathering at Culloden Moor. Culloden. I fancied there was something about that name that foretold a great victory— no matter that the ground was like a tabletop! And when the Battle of Culloden was over, Leofwin and I could ride home together to Ballachulish. When we got there, Big Archibald's leg would no doubt be healed, and the cabbage in Glenisha's patch would be tiny, pale-green buttons, and life would go on as before.

12

I snugged my wool cap around my ears to hide my hair and when I held my plate out for a dry biscuit and a spoonful of boiled barley, I was served just like any other soldier. I lowered myself into the damp heather among my new companions and studied them while I ate.

Oh, the plucky Highland army was not at all what I'd dreamed it would be!

The men who were gathered on the heather all around me were harried and tired. Their skins were blue with cold, yet they had no warm scarves to keep the chill off their necks, nor any good boots for their feet. When we'd finished our meager meal, my companions flipped their soiled plates into their haversacks, rolled themselves into their tartans, and turned themselves up to the sky to sleep with mouths open like sorry black holes in their weary faces.

I was nearly asleep myself, my coat pulled tight around me for I'd lost my tartan along with my cooking pot, when the call came: "Rise up, men! Up with you now, all you brave lads! We march to Nairn this very night and will take the Duke of Cumberland by surprise!" I knew from studying my map until I knew it by heart that Nairn was at least twelve miles away, on the Moray Firth, and would take several hours to reach. Worse, it would delay my search for Leofwin.

"Quite a party it'll be, wouldn't you say?" grumbled the man who'd been sleeping near a stone wall a few feet from me. He yawned mightily, and I observed that many of his teeth were missing. On his crest badge there was a raven perched on a blue rock, which told me its wearer was a follower of the MacDonells of Glengarry. "Party?" I echoed, annoyed. I was not at Culloden for anyone's party.

"Aye, you heard right. The Duke of Cumberland celebrates his birthday tomorrow. He's twenty-five years old come the dawn, and I'll wager his men got an extra ration of cheese and a few ounces of brandy this night in honor of the event. No doubt our prince has decided there'll be no better time to fall on the enemy than when they're happy and reeling and never dreaming of death!"

But it was nearly eight o'clock in the evening before the march finally got underway. We left a few men on Culloden Moor to tend small campfires that were scattered all across the heather to give the impression the whole army was still camped there. The man who'd slept against the wall beside me rode a pony that was lame in its right front shoulder and soon he cast an appreciative eye on Sionnach.

"A fine horse you've got there, laddie," he observed.

"It's a gift," I informed him quickly, "given to me by my brother, for we've always been as close as two brothers can be. He's here to fight for Prince Charlie, too," I added. "You might even have seen him. He's a tall lad, called by

96

the name of Leofwin. He has yellow hair and rides a High-land pony rather like your own."

My new acquaintance shook his head. "In war all men are apt to look alike." He frowned. "Name was Leofwin, you say? And what's yours, laddie?"

I was not likely to answer Mary Hadder MacColl! "Hadder," I replied, grateful that it was not a name that brought to mind a person who'd wear green silk shirts or cameo brooches.

"A good one," my marching companion agreed, "a plain name with strength and courage in it—and you'll need both before this night is over."

All the men who marched or rode around us did so un-happily. None of us had had more than a biscuit and a spoonful of barley to prepare us for the journey, and it was not enough to put a spring in one's step. We were able to cover no more than two miles in an hour, so when we neared Nairn at last, the sky was beginning to lighten in the east and was heavy with the promise of a cold spring rain.

Now that I was soon to be in battle I began to wonder what it would be like and was disappointed when our next orders were whispered from mouth to mouth down the line. "Hssst! Turn back! Hssst! Go back to Culloden Moor!"

The toothless Glengarry man who'd ridden all night by my side was put out of sorts by the orders. "Turn back?" he echoed indignantly. "When we have the enemy almost in our grip? Look there, lad," he instructed, and I followed his pointing finger with my glance. I was certain I could see the white sailcloth tents of the duke's encampment and the occasional twinkle of a lantern pricking the frosty darkness. A moment later I heard the English battalion drums beat out a reveille and sleepy Sassenach voices called out to one another through the early-morning gloom.

"But it's already too light for a surprise attack," someone close at hand told us.

"That's what comes of having an army that's too tired and hungry to march quickly," my friend retorted. "We're all paying now for the fact that Prince Charlie never gets his food wagons to the front lines where they belong. No army, not even a Highland one, can march forever on an empty belly!"

When we rode back over the road we'd just traveled along, my companion slumped in his saddle, his chin low on his chest, too disgusted to complain anymore. As the morning grew lighter, I could see around me men whose clan badges told me they were Camerons or Stewarts or MacIntoshes. "A few more hours and victory might've been ours!" groused a soldier with yew in his bonnet to proclaim his attachment to Clan Fraser.

After we'd dismounted at Culloden Moor, my friend recovered his voice. "I had a vision last night, lad," he confessed. "I saw fish scales in my hair." He paused and looked at me to see if I understood what he meant. I did, but I waited for him to go on. "It means I'll die soon, lad." It was true, so I could not tell him what had happened to me.

If a spark from a fire alights on your coat but does not burn, it is another omen of death. Just such a spark lit on my coat only two nights before. I left it there, hoping it would burn. When it didn't, I blew on it until finally a tiny flame came to life and ate a hole in my coat. I leaned against Sionnach and inspected the hole again. Aye, it was still there! I hoped it meant I had turned aside an ill omen, but

I knew there was no way for my companion to undo a vision of fish scales in his hair.

I flinched when he took my arm and pinched it, not from the pain but from the fear he might discover it was a lass's arm he had hold of, not a lad's. "With death so close, it's a pity we cannot change our coats when the wind blows from the other side," he sneered.

"We're not Campbells," I reminded him coolly, "nor so wily we'd send one son to fight for King George and the other to fight for King James as some have done."

We settled ourselves behind a stone wall that ran at an angle across the moor and gave us some shelter from the strong northeast wind. Below the wall, I could see men from Clans Stewart and Fraser and Farquharson but still caught no glimpse of anyone with hair as yellow as gorse or a set of fine shoulders that belonged to Clan MacColl. But I was weary and could look no more; I tied Sionnach so that he could graze and lay down to rest.

Three hours later I was waked by the rain that had begun to fall cold and hard, driven by the wind that came off the sea near Nairn. I was chilled, but the sight I next beheld cooled my blood far more quickly than the driving rain. To the east I could see the coats of the English soldiers, bright as poppies in the stern gray light of morning, and could hear the steady roll of their drums. We of the Highlands had failed to meet our enemy at Nairn, but they had not failed to meet us on Culloden Moor.

The enemy horsemen, their mounts either black or bay, not one horse over fifteen hands in height and each sporting a short, docked tail, faced us across the moor. Their battalion banners of crimson and silver and green and gold were bent forward by the wind that was thickening with sleet. The roll of the English drums was unrelenting, about seventy-five beats to the minute, counterpointed by the musical jingle of their bridle chains and spurs. Most amazing of all, the sound of the enemy approach was overlaid by the skirl and skriegh of bagpipes!

"Aye, those *are* bagpipes you hear!" My friend grimaced. "It's the Campbells, who else? They'd commit any crime against a fellow Scot for one small favor from an English king!"

On our enemy's right came great shire horses to pull their mounted guns. Birds spilled out of the heather at each step of those hooves that were as big as the lid of a cabbage pot, and behind the shire horses came the bread wagons. "The English travel with a four-day supply of rations," my companion said with a groan. Our stomachs churned at the mention. I hadn't tasted meat for ten days, and had eaten nothing at all since my biscuit hours earlier.

Stitched across the battalion banners that moved toward us was the insignia of each, and my companion identified them for me. "A dragon for Howard's, a lion for Barrel's, and a white horse for Wolfe's," he said. But it was the battlefield itself that made him wrathful.

"Is our prince mad?" he demanded, as if I had the answer. His lips were blue with chill and he brushed rain out of his grizzled eyebrows. "For a rowdy Highland brawl we need rough country, terrain that would make it hard for the English to position their guns." He turned a gray, rheumy eye on me as if seeing me for the first time.

"Not only that, our army seems terribly young and inexperienced this time around. Worse even than in the Rising of the Nineteen."

I let my glance slide away from his. "And *you* are younger than most, lad," he accused.

"Young does not mean I am without courage," I objected. "If my brother is old enough to fight, then so am I. We are only two years apart in age," I lied, neatly shaving two years off the truth.

"And you say your brother's got yellow hair?" my friend murmured and pulled on the end of his nose as if that might jog loose a memory.

"Aye, and I'd have joined him sooner except that Glenis —my mother, that is—needed help at home." My lies were piling up faster than I could count.

"You said your brother's name was—"

"Leofwin. Leofwin MacColl, and he—"

"MacColl?" my companion mused and thoughtfully fingered the raven on his crest badge. "Long ago, I knew a man named Archibald MacColl. He was young then and had a yellow-haired wife named Barbara and a pair of bairns who rolled around his yard as fat as pups. One of the bairns was a boy and the other was—" He reached out carefully and lifted my cap. "—a girl," he finished softly. He leaned so close that I could see the red lines in his tired eyes. "Do not worry, lass," he said. "Your secret is safe with me. And truth to tell, I'm not surprised that Archibald of the Strong Blows would raise himself a daughter who'd run away to war!"

I recognized the prince the moment he rode past us about eleven o'clock in the morning. He was long through the body, just as Leofwin had told me, and rode a lively gray gelding. His coat was tartan and his vest was buff; he had a white silk cockade in his hat and a curved sword in a scabbard that flapped against his thigh. He sat his horse easily, not at all like that poor bumpkin David Forbes, and I imagined I could see why ladies in the streets of Edinburgh threw kisses at him.

I searched the faces of the men around the prince for a glimpse of Leofwin, but he was nowhere to be seen. Across the moor, Cumberland's men had begun to form their lines, and I knew there was not much time left to look for my brother. When next I looked across the moor it was to see the duke had positioned his three-pound guns, ten of them in all.

One by one, the men of the Highland army began to rise out of the heather and a few began to pull off their tartans and tie their kilts between their thighs. Horses were being tied away from the field of battle, for Highlandmen always fought on foot. I realized I must find a safe place for Sionnach, too.

The prince's left wing was made up of MacDonalds; the center was held by the Frasers and MacLeans and Clan Chattan. The right was led by a mixture of Camerons and Stewarts and that was where Leofwin ought to be, for in battle we MacColls always rode beside the Stewarts. Yet I still saw no sight of the one who was supposed to have led Clan MacColl into battle in Big Archibald's place.

An awful suspicion rose up in me. What if Leofwin had run away? Or had never left Edinburgh? At this very moment he might be on a boat headed for the colonies. If he was not at Culloden Moor to uphold the honor of Clan

MacColl, I thought with sudden bitterness, then I would rather that he be dead.

"Claymore! Claymore!" my companion muttered under his breath, oblivious to my concerns. A claymore is a short, broad sword used by a Highlander in one-to-one combat, and when the cry "Claymore!" is given, it is a signal to proceed into battle. "The English guns are not primed yet, their lines are not in order. Now is the time to attack—*now!*"

"When the Lord made time, He made plenty of it," I tried to joke, but the old adage did not make my companion smile. We could see the prince counseling with his advisors on a slight rise of ground well out of range of the duke's cannons. "I just hope his highness manages his war better than he manages his bread wagons," my friend groaned.

The duke's men let go a volley. A handful of clansmen in the front ranks of the Highland army went down. Still, there was no cry of "Claymore! Claymore!" The prince walked his gray horse back and forth, back and forth, but no order came. Then the MacIntoshes of Clan Chattan, whose ancestors were French and whose name meant clan of the cat, broke and ran toward the enemy lines, stripping off their tartans as they flew, their claymores raised high over their heads. Hard in their wake, his kilt drawn high between his strong thighs, came my brother, Leofwin MacColl.

Even in the driving, sleety rain his hair was bright as brass and his shoulders were leaner than I remembered. "There he is," I cried to my friend. "That's my brother! That's Leofwin!"

The duke's cannons let go another volley and then

another and clansmen in front of Leofwin were mowed down. But Leofwin ran on, his yellow hair lifted on the wind. I jumped up and so did my companion. But rather than run forward into battle, he seized me in both arms and dragged me backward.

"This is a battle that cannot be won, lass," he shouted in my ear, "and you were not meant to die here today!" He picked me up and hurled me bodily across Sionnach's red back. He clamped a gnarled hand over my knee.

"Fly away home, child!" he grated at me through clenched teeth. Before I could stop him, he stripped the reins out of my hands so they hung loose and useless and slapped Sionnach hard on the rump.

Sionnach's wild leap carried me not into battle but away from it. Over the stone wall we went, across a ditch, and into a boggy patch, and then past a solitary stone house. I tried to catch hold of the reins but they escaped my grip each time. We'd flown northwest more than a mile when I felt the saddle start to slip. I kicked my feet free of the stirrups and dove headlong into the heather.

Sionnach halted as soon as he felt me go and stood over me with legs braced wide on either side of me, as if to shield me from harm. I crawled out from under his belly and felt my bones. They seemed to be all of a piece. I stood up, tightened the cinch, and mounted. I judge that we must be nearly two miles away from the battlefield, but the wind that blew toward me was laden with so much sulphur smoke that it colored the mist yellow, and its stench made me pinch my nose shut. Even so, I could hear the bold *pibroch* of the Camerons float back to me:

104

"You sons of dogs, of the breed, O come here on flesh to feed!"

I turned Sionnach east into the sleet, toward the battle that waited for me.

No more than an hour could have passed from the moment Clan Chattan broke for the English lines until I breasted a slight rise of ground on the northwest edge of Culloden Moor. One hour; 60 minutes; 3600 seconds.

But for as far as I could see, Highland clansmen lay four deep on the muddy heather. Thin ribbons of smoke rose from the bodies where ball and grapeshot had lodged. Sionnach trembled between my knees and kept his head raised high to avoid breathing the stink of gunpowder.

The rain continued to fall lightly, but now the enemy guns were silent. I slid off Sionnach's back and walked among the men of the clans who lay dead beside their sons and their sons' sons. "Won't it be a great day when we take Scotland back for the Scots?" Big Archibald had cried with anticipation. But that is not what had happened.

I walked slowly, hoping I would not recognize any of the fallen. I had not gone far before I came upon my Glengarry friend. He'd known Big Archibald; he'd discovered that I was a lass, not a lad . . . but the only thing I'd ever learned about him was that he wore a raven badge and rode with the MacDonells. Now it was too late ever to know more. Next to him lay a boy about my age who would never get older than he was today. His blue bonnet and badge of thistle told me that once he'd belonged to Clan Stewart.

I stopped counting the fallen. I no longer looked at them, either, at their torn limbs and bleeding faces and sightless eyes. Yet I walked on as if in a dream, drawing closer and closer to the enemy lines that barred the road to Nairn. Then, as if I'd known exactly where I'd find him, I came upon my brother. Then, oh, then I found Leofwin. . . .

13

How lightly my brother rested on the muddy heather, as if he did not intend to remain there long, but perhaps only to nap for moment and then to be up and off to tend to matters that mattered more!

His face was turned up to hold the weight of the cold gray sky, and even in the flat light of midday his hair gleamed as bright as brass and still curled sweetly behind his ears. I knelt at his side. Oh, he was gone, and I knew it, but I was compelled to look one last time into the eyes that once had been as blue as Barbara MacDonald's.

Leofwin stirred under my gaze.

"Oh, Leofwin, I thought you were—"

"I am, Haddie, I am," he whispered so softly I could scarcely hear the words. His eyes were two clear, open, blue windows only inches from my own. He smiled. "Somehow I am not surprised . . . that my last sight on this earth would be . . . to see you here on Culloden Moor . . . my dear, fierce Haddie!"

"Don't talk," I urged, as if I could yet save his life by

making him save his words. "It's not too late," I rattled on. "I have Sionnach close by. I'll get you away from this place. We'll go back to Ballachulish. We'll be safe there. Everything will be all right!"

"No, it won't, Haddie . . . it's too late for that . . . but I want you to promise. . . ."

"Anything, Leofwin. Anything!"

"Leave the Highlands, Haddie . . . this was our last rising . . . go away to the colonies, Haddie, and make a new beginning . . . remember, it's what I always wanted to do. . . ."

"I'll go, Leofwin," I promised. "We'll go together! But there's something I want to tell you, Leofwin. There's something you have to know. Leofwin?"

He didn't answer me. Slowly, slowly, the blue color seemed to fade from his eyes, leaving them as bleak and gray-colored as the skies over the moor. I took hold of his hand. "Leofwin?" I prompted. "Leofwin?" There was no answer. He would never hear me call his name again.

What had happened was so huge that I was grateful to be able to perform small, ordinary acts. I pressed Leofwin's eyes closed with my thumbs. I crossed his hands over his breast. I closed his muddy sark at his throat. I ought to have wept, but no tears came. My heart should have been breaking; instead, it was a dark, burrowing animal in the middle of my chest. I'd wanted to tell Leofwin I'd loved him all my life. I'd tried to tell him once before, the day he came home to Ballachulish, leading a red horse by a pair of plain leather reins. He hadn't wanted to listen then. And now . . . now he couldn't.

108

I could see the English soldiers advancing toward me across the moor, their coats as bright and cheerful as poppies in the falling rain. They walked slowly and their voices were genial. They fired their rifles into the bodies of the fallen clansmen as they came, or struck the wounded with their swords. "They will give us no quarter," Leofwin had warned. Their only task now was to write the final chapter to the war Big Archibald and I had wanted so much.

I crawled away from Leofwin's side and made my way back to where Sionnach stood ground-tied. I took hold of the stirrup on the red fox's left side and let him drag me slowly off the field. As soon as we were out of range of the English rifles, I mounted. We turned southwest, toward Ballachulish.

Only two hours earlier I had suspected Leofwin had not been true to the honor of Clan MacColl. In revenge for something I'd imagined, I had wished him dead. The un-examined life is not worth living, my brother had tried to tell me. Now he was gone—and I had the rest of my life to examine mine.

It was Big Archibald, not Glenisha, who welcomed me at the gate when I returned to Ballachulish.

My father's stay at the infirmary in Oban had left him pale, and his fiery mane was even more bestreaked with gray than it'd been when he went away. His left trouser leg, where once there'd been a limb as thick as a tree trunk, now was folded up and pinned to keep its emptiness from flapping.

"Leofwin?" He spoke the name first as a question, then as a long, tired sigh: "Ah, no, not Leofwin, not Leofwin. . . ."

"Aye, he fell with all the others," I told him. I could say the words but still could not feel their pain. My father's broody black glance slid past me. "My first bairn," he murmured into the air, "my only son." He passed his trembly fingers along his cheek and I waited for him to go on, but those six words were the only ones my father ever uttered about Leofwin. Big Archibald of the Strong Blows might not have been at Culloden, but something in him died there, too.

Glenisha waited for me in the doorway. Wise, good old

110

Glenisha! She simply opened up her arms to me and cradled me in them, unmindful that the top of her head came only to my chin. Later, the first meal the three of us shared was a common one, for without able men in Ballachulish to gather meat, the women and children who'd been left behind lived on vegetables and berries and fish. But I was grateful; we are together, I told myself, and that is all that matters.

I found out very soon that I was wrong. Leofwin, who'd been right about so many things, was right about the fate the Sassenachs had in store for us after we'd been vanquished.

The smoke from their cannons had scarcely cleared from Culloden Moor before the English ran off all our herds of dark, long-horned cattle. We were told that henceforth none of our lands could be passed from father to son nor inherited by any clan member. No fire could ever be lit again on a hilltop to call the men of a clan together; in fact, clansmen were forbidden from gathering in groups of more than three. We could nevermore possess a weapon, not even anything as small as a dirk. We could not wear our plaids; we were prohibited from playing our pipes or telling stories around a ceilidh fire. Not only did our property pass to the English but our customs as well, for victory had been theirs.

But most terrible of all: the men who'd fallen at Culloden had to remain there. The English buried our clansmen in mass, unmarked graves. Leofwin would never come home again.

Once upon a time, Big Archibald would've been so outraged by such punishment that his curses would've filled our great hall like a wrathful cloud, and he would've beaten his fists raw on our whitewashed walls. That's what the old Archibald would've done.

The new Archibald MacColl only turned away to dream into the fire. Perhaps at such a moment he returned to the sweet, white arms of Barbara MacDonald; maybe he remembered the starry winter night when his only son had been born. Now, my father, who'd never allowed me a gesture of fondness, was so bemused that he let me tease the snarls from his coarse red-gray hair every morning and let me lay a shawl on his shoulders when the evening air was cool.

"Grief has made him an old man before his time," Glenisha mourned.

"It's not grief only for Leofwin that's made him old," I answered. "It's for everything. For the long, bright fall of the clans, for the silent pipes, for all the things that couldn't last forever." So, one August evening when Big Archibald took his crutch under one arm and went to walk on the moor, we let him go quietly, alone.

When Glenisha sent me to fetch him later, I found my father resting beside the path which led down to the loch, his back against one of his favorite trees. He waited for me with his gaze directed across the water. I looked with him before I called him to come home, for I wanted to share with him the sights that once had lighted his blood and mine like a fever—the blue tumble of the mountains of Glencoe on our right, the peaks of Ardgour on our left, the silvered waters of Loch Linnhe before us.

Yet I was not surprised to take my father's hand in mine a moment later and feel his fingers cool against my own. Death had not come for him during the flurry and frenzy of battle as he had wished, but it had not ignored Big Archibald of the Strong Blows.

Jamie MacKenzie and Glenisha and I carried Big Archibald home to the White Tower and wrapped him in his bold red-and-black tartan. Let the Englishmen complain! "His plaid is now only a winding-sheet," I would tell them if they harried me about my choice.

In a different day, we would have rowed my father out to the Isle of Coll and would have laid him to rest beside his ancestors. In this new, strange time, we had to content ourselves with scraping away some thin soil until we struck rock, then placing his body in a shallow grave. I weighted my father's eyes with two silver coins that I took from Barbara MacDonald's wedding chest, then Jamie MacKenzie and I piled stones over him until we'd built a cairn that was level with the brass buckle at my waist.

Jamie MacKenzie reached for my hand to soothe me when our grim chore was finished, but I pulled myself quickly away. "Save your charm for a lass who'll appreciate it more," I told him. I knew I could remain strong only if I held onto my hard and bitter heart as if it were a precious jewel. I motioned him to be gone, and Glenisha, too. I wanted a few moments alone with Big Archibald, for they'd be the last ones we'd ever share.

"I can see our White Tower from where you rest," I told my father, and I was sure that he could hear my words.

113

"It's as lovely today as it's always been, but the English soldiers are swarming through the Highlands, Father, and they are scowdering the houses of all the rebels. None are to be spared. So tomorrow, Father, I will do what I know you'd want me to do." I took a deep breath before I went on.

"Tomorrow, Father, I will put a torch to the White Tower myself," I told him. Until I shaped my revenge in words, I had not known the form it would take. Now I saw the flames leap up and turn to ash everything we'd once held dear. "No one will ever again sleep in your fine box bed, Father. No one will ever eat a meal off your good oak table. No one will ever view Loch Linnhe from one of your tall windows. But I promise you on my honor that no Sassenach will have the satisfaction of torching your house himself!"

I was certain that I heard my father answer in his rich, booming voice of old, "Well done, Hadder MacColl! You were always my bonny Highland lion, the daughter of my heart!" What I could not tell Big Archibald was that when my deed was done and the White Tower was a smoldering pile of ash and rubble, Glenisha and I would leave the Highlands forever.

The next morning, Glenisha packed a pot with the last two cabbages left in the garden. We loaded barley into a sack from the cupboard against the wall. We wrapped a dozen golden herring, dried and sweetly smoked, in a square of oiled paper.

When that was done we went into our bedrooms and

each of us made a bedroll out of woolen blankets. Glenisha packed her old coat but did not take the plaid cape she'd rescued from the clutches of the tinker, for tartan was now illegal. I folded up my coat trimmed with lion's fur but left behind my buckled shoes.

The time to leave came so quickly, like the sun from behind the clouds! Sionnach stood saddled in the yard. Once again, his slim red legs were thickened with mud and straw; his mane and tail were clotted with burrs. Then, as Glenisha and I were about to step from my father's house, I lifted up a jar that held oil that we used to fill our lamps in the evening.

I poured oil across the oak table, splashed it across Barbara MacDonald's green-and-blue-and-gold tapestries, drenched the wooden sills of the windows.

"What are you doing?" Glenisha cried. I kept pouring.

"Stop!" she shrieked. "Stop this at once!" She seized my hand, and I was astonished by the vigor of her grip.

"I am going to put a torch to everything," I shouted and shook off her hand. "The English will not have the pleasure of doing it for me!"

Glenisha's face, only inches from my own, was bright with wrath. "Is your head so thick, cheelie, that you've learned nothing from everything that's happened?" she hissed back. "You cannot destroy the life you once loved! If you try, it's the same as putting a dirk in your own heart!"

I stared at her.

"When will you be satisfied, Mary Hadder MacColl?" she ranted on. "Leofwin is gone. Big Archibald, too. But leave this house standing in the sunlight, whole and all of a piece, as it's stood for two hundred years! The English might well decide to leave it that way, too. And who knows? Maybe someday it will harbor another Highland heart as brave as your own!"

Glenisha's words flew past me and collided with the walls we whitewashed each springtime before we went to the shielings. The dark stain in front of the fireplace still marked the spot where I'd thrown a piece of venison long ago. Lamp oil shimmered on Big Archibald's fine oak table, dripped off the tapestries on the wall, soaked into the windowsills.

The unexamined life is not worth living, Leofwin had tried to tell me. I had not wanted to listen. We Highlanders got our hearts mixed up with our history, he'd said. We carried our grudges to our graves. Some of us could even be inspired to carry them beyond. I decided to listen to Glenisha. I set the oil jar on the hearthstone and together we walked through the door and let it close behind us.

I helped Glenisha onto Sionnach's back. She sat there, proud as the girl I used to be, and looked down at me with smiling eyes. "Where are we going?" she wondered, her temper all spent.

"To Edinburgh," I told her, "and after that, to the colonies." I took Sionnach's reins from Jamie MacKenzie. "Will I ever see you again?" he asked me. His black eyes were hopeful, and I realized for the first time that I might have liked him. "Not in this life," I answered with regret. I wished that he would reach for my hand again. He didn't, so I waved good-bye and led Sionnach down the road.

I imagined the White Tower growing smaller and

smaller behind me with each step that I took, saw the deserted cow pens, the barren cabbage patch, felt Jamie MacKenzie's warm black eyes fastened on the back of my neck. I did not turn around for one last long look of farewell.

We stopped early our first night. There was no need to cook a meal, for Glenisha had carried along with her some thick barley soup held in a sheep's bladder. After I'd set Sionnach to graze, we ate the soup cold with a dry biscuit. Then we spread our blankets over a mattress of heather that we'd gathered and slept with the wind sighing over our heads in its mellow way, *luff-win, luff-win*.

In the morning, we shared another cold biscuit that we'd spread with jam, drank a bit of lukewarm tea, and were on our way again. In the days that came after that, a curious thing happened: the farther we got from Ballachulish, the younger Glenisha seemed to be and the older I became.

I looked back at her once. The wind lifted her gauzy hair, which was like a baby's first fine, thin hair, and the edge of her cheek was not old but was smooth and soft instead. I touched my own face. It was drawn, and I massaged a tight line that ran from my mouth to my chin. "We aren't children anymore, Had," Leofwin told me that day in the forest. "We grew up, one day at a time." But did growing up bring so much pain to everyone, I wondered, or only to me . . . ?

I headed east, toward Glencoe. At Laroch, a dirty person with wild hair barred the road and refused to let us pass. "Whither goest thou?" he cackled at us and, being without a horse, cast an appraising glance at Sionnach. "To Edinburgh, sir, to join some friends," I answered politely. "That's your mother, lassie?" he demanded, pointing at Glenisha. When I left Ballachulish this last time, I left it as a girl.

"Aye, and not well either," I told him. "All her kin were lost at Culloden, you see. I am the only one left to care for her."

His small eyes lost their cunning at that name, Culloden. "It was a wretched business," he agreed. "We lost too many there. It was the fault of the prince, of course. He was a fool who could not holler 'Claymore!' when the need was clear. It was a bad day for the Highlands when he landed at Eriskay!"

Glenisha looked down. "We were all a party to the troubles, laddie," she corrected him, "all of us who were quiet when the clans marched away to war." He flushed and let us pass then, humbled by Glenisha's words. What would I have done if he hadn't? I asked myself. I had no dirk, for it was illegal now to carry even the smallest weapon. I would've had to take up a stone or stick, would've had to call up my old rage and fury—everything that Glenisha seemed to despise.

After Laroch, we passed Achnacone, which was once called the Field of the Dogs by the MacDonalds. We passed Signal Rock and Achtriachtan. In such places my mother might have walked when she was my age, her golden hair hanging loose, her eyes calm and smiling as mine never were. The road to Callander was narrow, and we went on to Bannockburn, where Robert the Bruce was victorious

over the English on a Sunday in June in 1314. A day later
we passed Falkirk and then, on the waters of the Firth of
Forth, we came to a sprawling, smoky mass lying beneath
the hot August sun. We had arrived in Edinburgh.

So many poor folk clogged the streets of the city that
Glenisha and I need not have worried that we would be set
apart by our poverty. Beggars and urchins in rags thronged
the alleyways as we dragged ourselves along and searched
for a street named Northbridge. David Forbes had told me
once that his father's house was small and white and had a
roof of thatch, but all I could see for miles were slums with
small, dark courtyards into which I'd have been afraid to
wander seeking directions.

At last a beggar pointed out the Northbridge Road to us.
It took us outside the city a bit, to where the houses were
not packed together as closely as sheep in a pen, and at last
we came to a small white one with a roof of thatch. I led
Sionnach around to the alley, where I found a small cow
shed and a garden enclosed by a low stone wall. I helped
Glenisha out of the red fox's saddle and left her to hold his
reins while I went to the back door. Oh, in the Highlands I
had been such a wild and vauntie lass! But in Edinburgh I
was no better than any other beggar.

The girl who opened the door to me was not the Elizabeth
Forbes who had lived in my imagination.

This one did not powder her nose but had a wealth of
pale freckles on her cheeks. Her mild gray eyes were fringed
with thick, light-brown lashes. Her nose was not long and
sharp but was snubbed prettily. She was smaller by a head

than I was, softly curved where I was still straight, and her hands were white and soft instead of brown and callused like my own.

"Why, Mary Hadder, it's you," she said, for she knew me as quickly as I knew her. She smiled, and I was ashamed that I saw no jealousy in the eyes that looked straight into mine. She reached for my hand with her soft, white one and drew me gently through the doorway.

15

The furniture in the Forbes' parlor was genteel and old. The curtains at the small windows were embroidered with clever needlework. I touched one of them. "Your brother told me that you liked crocheting and embroidery and such," I ventured. I wondered if that would be the only thing I could find to talk to her about.

Elizabeth Forbes nodded. "Yes, that's often what I did when my father and David and Leofwin—" she began, then lowered her glance and bit her lower lip. In the four months that had passed since Culloden, the names of the fallen clans had been published, so she knew of Leofwin's fate. "—when the gentlemen, that is," she went on, "studied and talked in the evenings." She lifted her glance to mine. "Those were such good times," she finished quietly.

Once it had made me bitter to suspect that she loved Leofwin. Now it bound the two of us together. "Your brother told me you liked to paint pictures, too," I murmured, for I could not yet speak Leofwin's name out loud. I looked about and on the table, the mantle, the walls were many small paintings. One was of a bowl filled with yellow flowers, another showed mild brown cattle grazing in a field, a third was of a loch in which the aching colors of an evening sky were reflected. All of the paintings were as calm and pretty as Elizabeth Forbes herself.

To realize that she was not the person I'd always imagined her to be made the parlor suddenly seem cramped and airless. "I left Glenisha and Sionnach in the alleyway," I gasped. "I'd best go tend to them." I bolted for the door. "Wait!" she called after me. "David will be home soon, and he can help you. I will fix a room for you and—" The rest of her sentence was chopped short when the door shut behind me.

I hoped that it would be hours yet before I had to face David Forbes. What I wanted most of all was to be alone—without Glenisha, even—so that I could nurse my bruised sense of the person I used to be. But when I flew down the garden path to the alley, I discovered that David had already arrived. He had settled Glenisha on a bench in the garden from which she admired the daisies and eyebrights that grew everywhere. He had unsaddled Sionnach and was about to start brushing the mud and burrs out of his red coat.

I ran past David and Sionnach and heaved myself face-down in the clean straw piled in the corner of the cow shed and cradled my head in my arms. "Oh, Hadder, you're safe now," I heard him say the moment he knelt at my side. "The rebellion's over, and soon things will be all right again."

Those were almost the same words I'd said to Leofwin. I rolled onto my back but kept my face turned away from David Forbes'. I could see that he'd hung my Spanish bridle on a peg in the wall. Its roses still looked as fresh as the ones that grew beside the Forbes' back door.

"The truth," I told him, "is that nothing is over. The rest of my life is just beginning, but even though I might live to be as old as Glenisha, I will always have to remember that Leofwin went off to fight in a war that he didn't believe in. All the bright things I loved are all behind me. I wish I were dead on Culloden Moor with my brother."

From where I lay, I could see Glenisha leave her perch on the garden bench to inspect some small flowers shaped like hearts that grew on a low bush. She needs only a cheelie to care for in order to be happy, I thought. I needed all the things I could never have again—Leofwin, Big Archibald, the White Tower.

David Forbes laid a forefinger against my cheek and turned my face to his. "There are lots of things that still matter, Mary Hadder MacColl!" he objected. I was startled by the fierceness in his voice. "For instance, you can have a place here with us in Edinburgh. It would make Leofwin so happy to know that you are safe—and Elizabeth can even teach you how to paint!"

Would that be me? I wondered. A person who painted clever little pictures . . . who crocheted edges on linen curtains . . . whose hands were smooth and white? No, that would never be me! At heart, I was still what I'd always been: a toe-rag, a wild child.

"I'm going," I told David Forbes softly without looking at him.

"Going?" he echoed. "Going where, Mary Hadder?"

He was not as quick to understand as Glenisha had been

123

when I told her I was going to war. David Forbes (I was doomed to always think of him as David Forbes!) rocked back on his heels in the straw and lifted my hand in his own. "To the colonies," I answered. " 'Go to the colonies, Haddie'—those were Leofwin's very last words to me. He told me once that it would be a good place to forget old grudges. I hope that he was right."

But along with not being meant for a life in Edinburgh, I was not meant to lie flat on my back in anyone's straw pile either! I scrambled to my feet and leaned against the rail of the little pen that held Sionnach and a small brindle cow with her new calf. Sionnach lipped up some oats that David had given him in a wooden trough, his eyes half-closed with contentment.

"The problem," I explained to David, "is that I have no money for boat passage to the colonies." I paused, then rushed on, for I did not want to think too long about what I must say next. "You see, Glenisha and I had to leave everything behind when we left Ballachulish. We only brought one thing with us that I can sell in order to get passage money. Only one thing. . . ." I smoothed Sionnach's red forelock over the star in his forehead and began to braid it as it was braided the first time I laid eyes on him.

David jumped to his feet, too, and stood beside me. "Maybe I can get some money, Hadder," he offered quickly. "You could repay me later when you're—"

I shook my head. "I didn't come all the way to Edinburgh to beg like a tinker," I told him briskly. I took a deep breath. "But if you will buy Sionnach from me, then Glenisha and I will be able to go to America. I know that

124

you would take good care of Sionnach and—" In spite of my hard heart, I began to choke. "And it would be easier to go, knowing he was in good hands," I finished in a thin, fleechy voice I hardly recognized.

"Oh, Hadder, maybe we can think of a better way, and then when you come back—"

I looked straight at David Forbes. "I can't ever come back, David," I said. "I was as loyal to the rebel cause as Big Archibald."

"I know you were, Hadder." He groaned. "But how I wish, oh, how I wish—" He made a clumsy half-circle of his arms, and I let myself step into the comfort that he offered. I laid my cheek against his. His shirt smelled faintly of the same lavender talcum that Elizabeth had used to perfume her letter to Leofwin.

In another time and in another country, I thought with astonishment, I might have been an ordinary girl in the arms of an ordinary boy! But David Forbes and I had been trapped in history just like Leofwin. If life in the Highlands had not been so fierce, I might even one day have worn a cameo at my throat and a green silk shirt might've lain as light as air against my skin! But because I was a Highlander, because I was Archibald MacColl's lion-hearted daughter, I had dreamed only of pulling thunder from the sky.

"What makes it all so hard," I heard myself confess against the curve of David Forbes' neck, "is that you were right about forever. It *was* a dangerous word. I know now that nothing lasts forever, not even the things you love the best."

David Forbes clamped his arms around my shoulders and shook me hard. "Nothing is ever lost if you can remember it, Hadder! You see, I believe there is another kind of forever, the kind made up of little pieces of now."

I held onto David Forbes as hard as he hung onto me. *Little pieces of now.* The now of the first time Leofwin and I rode into our forest . . . the now of seeing Sionnach come over the rise in the cart road, his red mane and tail filled with wind . . . the now of the instant I decided not to torch the White Tower—gathered together, could all those pieces make a different kind of forever?

"I have something else to tell you," I whispered in David Forbes' ear. "When you came to the Highlands, I thought you were a spy. Leofwin told me that you only wanted to be my friend. I found out too late that he was right." We stood a long time, locked in each other's arms. When I left Scotland, I knew I could also take away the now of our only embrace.

Every afternoon for a week, Glenisha went with Elizabeth to gather fresh flowers out of the garden, and their voices floating in the open window were like the mingled songs of two birds. We ate mutton and fish and warm oatmeal bread at the Forbes' supper table and afterward, Doctor Forbes, whose hair was as silvery as Glenisha's, would read to us about men like Plato and Aristotle and Socrates. Every night, Glenisha and I rested between smooth, clean linen sheets and were almost bewitched into believing such a life might go on without end.

Then one afternoon David Forbes came home with a plan

that would save me from having to sell Sionnach. Unbeknown to Glenisha and me, we had something else to sell. Ourselves.

"It's called indenture," David Forbes told us at the supper table that evening, "and this is how it works. You can get free passage on a ship that is bound for the colonies in exchange for the sale of your labor once you arrive there. You must sign a contract before you leave, of course. Later, that contract will be sold to someone in the colonies who wants to buy a servant."

A servant? A wild child from the Highlands would have to sell herself as a *servant?*

"But when the time of your indenture is over," David Forbes went on, "you will be a free person. Not only will you be free, you will be allotted a piece of land on which to make a new start in life. The king, you see, is anxious to settle people in the colonies while at the same time ridding himself of all who sympathized with the rebellion."

"This contract you speak of," I ventured in a small voice, "how long is it for? A year? Maybe only two?"

David Forbes' glance held mine. "The shortest contract that is granted is for four years, Hadder. You'll have to bind yourself for four years." Four long years—I'd be nineteen years old before I was free again, older by a year than Leofwin was when he fell at Culloden. "And what about Sionnach?" I asked feebly.

"There are no provisions in the contracts for indentured persons to take livestock to the colonies with them," David Forbes admitted. "But we can keep Sionnach safe for you here, Hadder. He's a young horse, only four or five years old. In another four years he'll only be nine—a prime age for a horse such as he is! And who knows? After your indenture is over and you have gotten your plot of land, maybe we can figure out a way to ship Sionnach to you. Cattle and sheep and goats are often shipped to the colonies, and I am sure a horse could be, too."

I folded my hands on the table. Glenisha waited for me to decide our fate, her face as trusting and eager as a child's. "Aye, we'll do it." I said. Two weeks later, after David Forbes made the proper arrangements, I signed my name to the indenture contract that lay before me. Glenisha set down a small *x* for her mark. I was almost glad that at last our destiny was sealed.

Ten days later, on the twelfth of September, a cart appeared on Northbridge Road in front of the Forbes' house. It had been called to carry Glenisha and me to the docks. David walked with Glenisha and me to the street, and as we stood there I wondered what it would be like to kiss him good-bye. I had never kissed anyone except my mother before, not even Big Archibald or Leofwin. Kissing, like forgiving, did not seem to come easily to the MacColls. But at the very moment I might've taken David Forbes' face between my two hands and kissed him on the lips, his sister came hurrying down the path toward us, her small white hands closed around a parcel wrapped in blue paper.

Elizabeth smoothed her gleaming, cared-for hair, and I couldn't help reaching up to touch my own. It was as wild and unruly as a moor pony's tail. "Open this when you are on the boat, Mary Hadder," she told me in her soft, quiet way, then added in a voice that had a crack in it: "We all loved him, you know." Although Leofwin's name had not once been mentioned, we all knew who she meant. Her eyes were shiny as she spoke of the person we would all go on missing our whole lives long.

I stuffed Elizabeth's gift in my pocket. I had saved the hardest good-bye of all until the very end.

I turned away from the cart and ran back to the tiny barn at the end of the Forbes' garden. Sionnach threw up his long, starred red head as I rushed in, and the sight of him there made me stop in my tracks. Oh, I wanted to leap onto his back, fly out of the garden and over the wall, down the cobbled streets of Edinburgh, and flee for the Highlands where I could be the person I was meant to be.

Maybe I could find a corrie in the high country where the red fox and I could live out our days. I would roll a boulder across its entry so that no one could ever disturb us . . . I would build a shelter of pine boughs . . . there would be grass enough for Sionnach to graze on . . . a stream filled with fish for us to drink from. When at last our lives were over, our bones would bleach in the summer sun and would turn to powder beneath the winter snows.

Sionnach studied me with glowing dark eyes. I laid my palm over the crisp white star in his forehead. "But it was never meant to be, was it, my fine red fox?" I asked him. He flicked an ear to let me know that he understood. "Oh, you were such a grand gift, the best any brother ever gave to a sister!" I laid my cheek against his silky neck and breathed deeply of the good, rich red smell of him. I hoped I could remember it all my life.

"Stay proud," I whispered. "Stay swift and keep your bold heart and don't let David Forbes make a common old cart horse out of you! And maybe someday you and I can be together again!"

I let him go and stood back. Any other time, Sionnach would've gone back to eating beside his new stablemate, the little brindle cow, but this time the red fox arched his neck longingly over the stall door, as loathe to let me go as I was to let him go. It would be bad luck, I decided, to call good-bye to him, so I simply turned and ran back down the garden path to where the cart waited for me.

Glenisha was already perched in it. I touched David and Elizabeth Forbes lightly on their shoulders, leaped into the cart beside my old minnie, and we were gone.

When Glenisha and I had settled ourselves snugly into the hold of the ship—it was dark and crowded, for there were many others who were fleeing the Highlands with us—she turned to me in a sudden, startled way, as if she could not quite remember where we were or how we'd gotten there. She put her quivery fingers against my face and traced my features as if she'd forgotten who I was, too.

To freshen her memory I whispered, "We're going to the colonies, minnie, don't you remember? In a few weeks we'll come to a harbor they call Boston, then we'll take up our new life."

"And afterward we'll come home again?" she asked plaintively. For Glenisha, just as for me, home would always be a tall white house with a blue slate roof beside the glassy waters of Loch Linnhe.

"No, Glenisha," I told her, "we won't ever come home again."

"Never again," she echoed. "Never again. . . ." She reached for my hand; her fingers were dry as parchment against mine. I searched about for something to distract her from the grimness of my message and remembered the gift from Elizabeth Forbes. I drew it out of my pocket.

"Shall we open this now?" I cajoled in the kind of high, light voice I might've used to wheedle a child like Ada Simpson. Glenisha nodded brightly, pleased. I was the minnie now, and she had become the cheelie.

I unwrapped the tiny parcel. In the nest of blue paper I found a painting that was no bigger than a plover's egg. It was the portrait of a boy with golden hair and eyes the color gentians would've envied. Glenisha took the picture from me and held it up to a shaft of light that came through the door of the hold.

"Aye, doesn't our own bonny lad look handsome!" she exclaimed. I dared not allow myself more than a single anguished glance, for it would be years before I could ever bear to look upon that face again.

Our ship began to move from the quay as the wind filled its sails and from the darkness around us a soft, weeping sound rose up. Our boat-mates were no more eager to leave Scotland than Glenisha and I were. The water lapped gently against the side of the ship and Glenisha whispered, "Tell me again what it was like when we all lived in Ballachulish."

She had in mind the story I had recounted to her every evening as we traveled from the high country toward Edinburgh. "Tell me about that place in the forest, cheelie,"

she urged. "You said you and Leofwin had a name for it—"
She tapped her forehead as she tried in her new, vague way
to remember that name. "You said it was—"

"The Forest of Forever," I filled in for her. I did not
want to go on. Glenisha prompted me by squeezing my
fingers, and I heard myself begin to tell her once more the
story that I understood at last was made up mostly of pieces
of now.

In that story there was a boy whose mother had given
him a name that meant to win love . . . there was a wild
girl who wore a coat trimmed with the fur of a Highland
lion . . . there was a tall red horse whose mane and tail were
filled with wind and stars. They all lived near a forest that
surrounded a dark pool where every autumn kelpies climbed
into golden boats and sailed away, as Glenisha and I were
about to do, to find the sun.

AFTERWORD

Only nine months after his arrival on the island of Eriskay, Prince Charles Edward Stuart was defeated in his attempt to take back the crown for his father, King James. The Battle of Culloden lasted less than one hour. When it was over, twelve hundred men from the Highland clans lay dead on the rain-soaked heather. The English army, ably commanded by the Duke of Cumberland, who was not only the same age as Bonnie Prince Charlie but was his cousin as well, lost but fifty soldiers.

The rebels who survived the Battle of Culloden were not allowed the honor of carrying away their dead to lay them to rest in the sweet green glens of the Highlands. Instead, the fallen were buried in mass graves, and among the gray headstones that today dot the length and breadth of Culloden Moor is one that reads simply:

The Battle of Culloden
Was Fought on This Moor
16th April 1746.

The Graves of the
Gallant Highlanders
Who Fought for
Scotland and Prince Charlie
Are Marked by the Names
of Their Clans.

The names of those clans still ring like bells in Scots history —MacDonald and MacLean, Fraser and Farquharson, Cameron and MacColl. Records of the battle show that eighteen MacColls, whose clan badge was the thistle, died at Culloden. Fifteen were wounded there. To escape the wrath of Scotsmen and Englishmen who had opposed Prince Charlie's rebellion, many Highlanders emigrated to the American colonies, where they sold themselves as indentured servants. In 1746, one of them was a fifteen-year-old red-haired girl. Her name was Hadder MacColl.